THI

Charlotte be
and grabbed
tightly.

'Oh, Tom

'OK, he's cute. But you're not going to take him along, are you, Charl?'

'I'll put him down in a sec, Tommy. I just wanted to see if I could pick him up. And pet him a little. *Ouch!*' She dropped the field mouse. 'Little devil *bit* me.'

'Hurt you, honey?' Tommy asked.

'No, just a little nip. Startled me, that's all.' She happened to look down again. 'Tommy! Look!'

The field mouse was running back, this time towards Tommy. It started to run up the leg of his trousers. He knocked it off with a hand, sent it rolling four or five feet. It came back to attack again – if attack was its intention. This time Tommy had kept his eyes on it, and was ready. His foot lifted and came down; there was a faint crunching sound. With the side of his shoe he kicked what was left of the field mouse off the path.

THE MIND THING

FREDRIC BROWN

Hamlyn Paperbacks

THE MIND THING

ISBN 0 600 36358 9

First published
in Great Britain 1979
by Hamlyn Paperbacks

Hamlyn Paperbacks are published by
The Hamlyn Publishing Group Ltd,
Astronaut House,
Feltham,
Middlesex, England

Set, printed and bound in Great Britain by
Cox & Wyman Ltd, Reading

CHAPTER ONE

The mind thing used his perceptor sense to test this strange and alien environment in which he found himself. He had no organs of vision or hearing, but his perceptor sense was something far better; he could 'see' all around himself, very clearly for about twenty yards, tapering to dim vision for another twenty or so, but his seeing was unimpeded by intervening objects. He could see the bark on the far side of a tree as plainly as that on the near side. He could see down into the ground as far and as clearly as in any other direction. His ability to sense vibrations extended even farther and was extremely acute within its range.

He could not only see but 'hear' worms burrowing in the ground under him; they were puzzling, for no such life form existed in any other world he knew of. But they seemed to offer no danger. Nor did a few small birds in the trees overhead. They were almost familiar; bird life tends to evolve along quite similar lines on all warm planets that have atmospheres dense enough to permit natural flight. (But what monstrous trees they perched in! They were several times as large as any he had ever known.) And there was a strange four-legged animal sleeping in a burrow, a tunnel in the ground which it seemed to have made for itself only about ten yards away.

Since the four-legged one was sleeping, the mind thing knew that he could enter into its mind, make it his host. But there seemed nothing to gain. Where there were small creatures there were almost certainly large ones, with more strength and brain capacity. Possibly even . . .

Yes! His second scanning of his surroundings showed him something he had not noticed on the first one. Lying in the grass a dozen yards away was a rusted broken-bladed jack-knife that had been thrown away or lost there. He didn't recognise it for a jack-knife, but whatever it was it was plainly an artifact. And an artifact meant intelligent life!

It meant danger, too. Intelligent life could be inimical, and he was small and vulnerable. He had to know more about the intelligent life form, preferably by catching its first specimen when it was sleeping, so he could enter its mind. He could learn more that way than by any amount of observation.

He was in an exposed position right beside what seemed to be a path. He had to get himself at least as far as the tall grass a yard away where he would be out of sight. Such concealment would be useless, of course, against his own kind or any other race that had perception instead of sight. But the chances were thousands to one that the intelligent creatures here, whatever they might be like otherwise, had only sight. He knew that on none of the thousands of known planets had both vision and the sense of perception developed side by side. One or the other, only. And here the birds and the small four-legged animal all had eyes.

He tried to levitate himself to move that yard, and found that he could not. He was not surprised. He had already suspected from several indications that this, compared to his own world, was a heavy-gravity planet. And his species, even on their own planet, had almost lost the power of levitation. Levitation was a strain, and since they all had hosts it was so much easier to have their hosts move them, when moving was necessary, than to levitate. An unused power diminishes as surely as an unused muscle atrophies.

So he was helpless, until and unless he could find a host

strong enough to move him. And the only creature *sleeping* nearby, the only one he could take over and make a host, was definitely too small, probably weighed about half what he did. Of course he could reduce his weight somewhat by *trying* to levitate while the four-legged—

Suddenly, at extreme range he perceived something, and concentrated all his attention in that direction. If danger was coming there wasn't time now to experiment with using the small animal to move him into concealment.

At first it was only vibration, vibration that could have been footsteps, footsteps of something relatively large. And there was another type of vibration that came through the air and not through the ground, that was like the sounds certain types of creatures, usually intelligent ones, who communicated vocally, used for that purpose. There seemed to be two voices, one higher in the vibration range than the other, talking alternately. Of course the words meant nothing to the mind thing, nor could he probe their thoughts; his species could communicate telepathically but only among themselves.

Then they came within range of visual perception. There were two of them. One was slightly larger than the other, but they were both big. Obviously they were members of the intelligent race, or *an* intelligent race, for they both wore clothing – and only intelligent races wear clothing, during a certain period of their development. They stood erect, and had two legs and two arms apiece. Also hands – and that would make them excellent hosts, but there was no time to think of that now. His problem was survival, until he could catch such a creature sleeping.

They were of a two-sexed species, he saw – for though he perceived their clothing his perception was not limited thereby; he could have studied their internal organs as readily as their nude bodies – and they were one of each sex. They were mammalian.

But the important thing was that they were coming closer, they were walking along the path and they would pass within one or two feet of him; they could hardly miss seeing him.

Out of desperation he grabbed at the mind of the only host available, the small four-legged one. He took no time to probe or study it; he started it scurrying madly out of its burrow. He'd have it intercept the two aliens. What would happen then he didn't know, but he had nothing to lose. He was less helpless with a small, weak host than with none at all. Perhaps, although it was unlikely, the tiny life form might be dangerous to the large strong life forms. Perhaps it was venomous or equivalently deadly in some other way. All over the galaxy there were planets on which some small life form was able, in one way or another, to terrorize larger creatures. It was at least equally possible that the two-legged creatures would look upon the little four-legged one as food and try to catch it to eat. In that case, he hoped the little creature could run as fast as they; if it could, he could have it lead them off the path for a while until they were safely past him. Then it would be safe to have them catch it and kill it.

It would have to be killed, or kill itself, in any case. Just as the only way he could enter a host was while it slept, the only way he could leave one was at the moment of its death. And this host was too frail and tiny a thing for him to want to use any longer than he had to stay in it.

Charlotte Garner stopped walking suddenly, and because she had her right arm linked with Tommy Hoffman's left he stopped too, so unexpectedly in his case that he almost went off balance for a second. He looked at Charlotte and saw that she was looking down at the path in front of them.

'Look, Tommy,' she said. 'A field mouse. And look what it's doing!'

Tommy looked. 'I'll be darned,' he said.

The field mouse, right in the middle of the path and not much over a foot away from them, was sitting up like a prairie dog. But quite unlike a prairie dog, it was waving its little front feet frantically, as though trying to signal to them. And its sharp little eyes looked directly up into theirs.

'I never saw one act like that,' Charlotte said. 'It acts as if it's *friendly*, not afraid. Maybe someone made a pet out of it, and then it got away – but still likes people.'

'Could be, I guess. I never saw one act like that either. Okay, Mousie, move along so we don't have to step over you.'

'Wait a minute,' Charlotte said. She'd already disentangled her arm from his. 'It's so tame I bet I can pick it up.'

Even before she'd finished saying that, Charlotte bent down, swept out a hand, and grabbed the field mouse gently but tightly. Charlotte was a very quick-moving girl, with fast reflexes. She had the field mouse before Tommy could protest (if he would have) or before the mouse could turn and run (if it would have).

'Oh, Tommy, he's cute.'

'Okay, he's cute. But you're not going to take him along, are you, Charl? You can't hold him while we–'

'I'll put him down in a sec, Tommy. I just wanted to see if I could pick him up. And pet him a little. *Ouch!*' She dropped the field mouse. 'Little devil *bit* me.'

The field mouse scurried away from them and off one side of the path and then, only about six feet away, stopped and looked back to see if they were chasing it. They weren't; they weren't even looking at it, and they hadn't moved.

'Hurt you, honey?' Tommy asked.

'No, just a little nip. Startled me, that's all.' She happened to look down again. 'Tommy! Look!'

The field mouse was running back, this time towards Tommy. It started to run up the leg of his trousers. He knocked it off with a hand, sent it rolling four or five feet. It came back to attack again – if attack was its intention. This time Tommy had kept his eyes on it, and was ready. His foot lifted and came down; there was a faint crunching sound. With the side of his shoe he kicked what was left of the field mouse off the path.

'*Tommy!* Did you have to—?'

His face was dark as he turned to her. 'Charl, that thing was crazy, attacking me twice. Listen, if it drew blood when it bit you we've got to get back to town fast. And take it with us, so they can check to see if it was rabid. Where'd it bite you, Charl?'

'On the b-breast, the left breast, when I held it close against me. But I don't think it drew blood – not through this sweater and a bra. It was more a pinch than a bite. It didn't hurt much, just scared me into letting go of it.'

'We'll have to check. Take off your— No, we're almost *there*. One minute won't matter, and somebody might come along here.'

He took her arm this time and strode ahead so fast that she almost had to run to keep up with him.

'Look, a turtle,' she said, a dozen steps on.

He didn't slow down. 'Haven't you played with enough animals this afternoon? Hurry, honey.'

Another dozen paces and they turned off the path, went around behind trees and bushes to the spot that they had discovered together and had made peculiarly theirs. It was a soft grassy spot screened from all directions by bushes, a perfect hideaway just far enough from the path so they couldn't even be heard there if they talked in normal tones of voice. It had all the privacy of a desert island and none of the latter's disadvantages. It was as sylvanly beautiful as it was secluded. And easily accessible, for young and healthy people to whom a two-mile walk each way was a pleasure and not a tiring chore.

They were young and healthy, and deeply in love.

Tommy Hoffman was seventeen and Charlotte Garner was sixteen. They had played together as children. They still went to school together and were now in the same grade, for Tommy, who didn't care much for schooling, had flunked a grade once, putting him back to Charlotte's level. They had each completed two years of high school.

They had fallen in love a year ago and six months ago had decided to get married. They'd talked to their families about it and had met no opposition except on the subject of when the marriage might take place. Tommy, who had just passed his seventeenth birthday, wanted them to quit school right away and get married. There would be no difficulties, he pointed out. Tommy's father was a widower and Tommy an only child; they lived in a quite large farmhouse (Mr Hoffman had been thinking ahead to a large family when he had built it), so there'd be not only room for Charlotte but for their children, if and when they had any. And Tommy, who knew a lot about farming already and wanted to be a farmer in any case, could help his father full time instead of part time; Charlotte would take over the house and between them they'd more than earn their keep. And that was the arrangement that would no doubt be made two years from now if they finished high school first, so why wait? What did a farmer want with a high school diploma? Mr Hoffman himself, Tommy pointed out, had had only a grade school education, and had done all right for himself. Besides, neither he nor Charlotte *wanted* to finish high school. They didn't hate school, exactly, but they didn't think they were getting anything out of it either. What good would history or algebra do a farmer or a farmer's wife?

As usual in such discussions, when they are amicable on all sides, a compromise was reached. They didn't have to finish high school and lose two years. If they waited one year, continuing school meanwhile, until Tommy was eighteen and Charlotte seventeen, Tommy's father and Charlotte's parents would give them consent to quit school and get married.

That had been six months ago and now they had only another six months to wait. In another sense they had quit waiting a month ago. They had held out (or Charlotte had) until the day a month ago when, walking through the woods, they had found this tiny, secluded paradise. And that day the weather had been too perfect, the place too beautiful, the kisses too wonderful, and the petting too passionate; biology had taken over. There had been no tears or regrets; for a first experience (for both of them) it had been unusually wonderful. Of course, having no standard of comparison, they didn't know it was unusually wonderful; just that it was very wonderful indeed. Nor had they any regrets, then or since, on moral grounds. They had been brought up to believe that sex outside of marriage was wrong, but *this* wasn't wrong. They were going to be married anyway, weren't they, as soon as they could? Meanwhile they could consider themselves already married in the eyes of God – and if there is a God who cares about such things, no doubt he did so consider them. They were very much in love.

This was the third time they'd been back here since. But this one didn't start like the others, because of the field mouse.

'Quick, Charl,' Tommy said urgently. 'Peel off that sweater. I'll unhook your bra while you're doing it. And if there's the slightest break in your skin where that – that thing bit you, we'll have to get back, *run* back.'

Her sweater was off, then her bra. They both examined her left breast. It was a very nice, very shapely breast; so was her right one. And one was as clear and unmarked as the other.

'Thank God,' Tommy said. He sighed deeply with relief. 'Does it hurt at all?'

She pressed an experimental fingertip just above the

nipple. 'Just enough so I can tell where it was.' She lowered her hand and smiled at him. 'You might kiss it and make it well. If you need an excuse.'

Tommy didn't need an excuse. And they both knew that what was going to happen would be at least as wonderful as the other times, and maybe a little more so because of reaction from the scare they'd had.

And wonderful it was; but this time, although they didn't know it, something was different.

This time something watched them, something whose equivalent of vision was not blocked by intervening trees and bushes. Something more horrible (although dispassionately so) than anything either of them had ever conceived in nightmare.

CHAPTER TWO

The mind thing watched avidly. Not because of prurience; he would not have understood the meaning of the word. He had no sex himself; the pronoun *he* being used only because *it* becomes very awkward when repeatedly used as a personal pronoun. His species reproduced by fission, by one creature dividing himself and becoming two, as do only lower life forms, such as bacteria, on Earth.

But he watched as eagerly as though his interest were prurient, because of a sudden hope, once he saw and understood what they were doing. Now he felt hopeful of acquiring a suitable host, and soon. He knew, from his knowledge (some first hand, some acquired) of a thousand worlds which held creatures that, like these, were of two sexes and performed the sex act in at least a somewhat similar manner, that they had a strong tendency to sleep after performing their sex act. Not because it physically exhausted them, but because the intelligent species so sexed found themselves emotionally exhausted, and contentedly replete.

If either of them slept, he had a host. If they both slept, he decided, he would choose the male since he was definitely the larger and stronger of the two. Quite probably the more intelligent as well.

After a while they relaxed and were motionless for a moment and he began to hope. Then they moved again, kissed a few times, murmured a few things. But then, relaxing in a somewhat different position, they were quiet again.

The female slept first, and he could have entered her, but the male had his eyes closed and his breathing was slow and regular; obviously he was on the verge of sleep, so the mind thing waited.

Then the male slept, and the mind thing entered his mind. There was a brief but terrible struggle as the ego, the essence, the part of the mind that was Tommy Hoffman, fought back. There was always such a struggle in taking over an intelligent creature. (It was negligible in the case of an animal; it had taken him only a micro-second to enter the small four-legged one less than an hour ago.) But the more intelligent the species the harder the struggle was; it varied, too, with the degree of intelligence of the individual within the species.

In this case it took him about a second, average for a moderately intelligent creature. Then he had Tommy's body. The whatever-you-want-to-call-it that was Tommy Hoffman was still there, but locked up and helpless, unable to use its own body or its own senses. The mind thing had it, and it could obtain release now only through death. Tommy's death, or the mind thing's.

The mind thing now had all of Tommy's memories and all, such as it was, of his knowledge. But he was going to take time to assimilate all of that, make sense of it, and make his plans from it. First things came first.

And the first thing was to get himself – his own body, into a safe place of concealment. Before some other man or men (he had Tommy's vocabulary now to think with) might come along and harm or destroy it.

He let everything else go and searched Tommy's thoughts and memories for a good hiding place, and found one. Half a mile deeper in the woods was a cave in a hillside. A small cave, but a secret one. Tommy had found it years ago, when he was a boy of nine, and had thought of it as *his* cave and had never shown it to anyone else; to his knowledge no one else knew of its existence. Besides, it had a sandy floor.

Very quietly so as not to awaken the girl (he could have strangled her, of course, but that would be an unnecessary complication; he had no empathy for lesser creatures but neither did he kill wantonly), he got up and started for the path. Since time might be important – someone else might come along that path at any time – he didn't have his host dress. Tommy wore only a pair of blue socks; his other garments – shoes, shorts, trousers, and a shirt – lay in a pile beside where he had been lying.

Just before he parted the bushes to leave the secluded spot he looked back to make sure the girl was still sleeping. She was, her young body completely nude. Not even socks in her case, since she'd been wearing barefoot sandals to begin with. He knew, from Tommy's mind, why they hadn't put their clothes on after the act. The sun had felt pleasantly warm on their naked bodies, and besides Tommy had hoped that after a short nap – they knew one or the other would waken within half an hour – he would be able to – 'go another round' was the phrase that had been in Tommy's mind. Obviously these creatures got considerable pleasure out of copulation. And also, although they always wore clothing except in privacy, from the sight and touch of one another's naked bodies.

At the path he picked himself up and started off at a trot in the direction of the cave he had found in Tommy's mind, the cave that would be his hiding place, at least for a while.

Probing Tommy's mind, he learned the answer to something that had puzzled him – why Tommy and the girl had seen him but had not stopped to investigate. Superficially, seen from above, he somewhat resembled an Earth (he knew the name of the planet now) creature called a turtle. To a casual glance he was a turtle about five inches long, with its feet and head pulled into its shell. Turtles were slow-moving and unintelligent; they did not bother humans, and humans seldom bothered them. True, they were edible – the concept and taste of turtle soup came to him – but unless he was hunting turtles a human would be unlikely to pick up and take home a single one only his size; it would weigh about two pounds, about his own weight, but it would yield only a few ounces of edible meat; not enough, except to a starving man, to be worth the trouble of killing and dissecting it.

That accidental resemblance had saved him. That and the actions of the field mouse while it had been his host. What he had done with the field mouse had been the right thing, if for the wrong reasons; another lucky accident. They had not been afraid of it nor would they have chased it off the path. But by biting the girl when she had picked it up and then attacking the boy when the girl dropped it, it had aroused fear that it had had something called rabies and that it might have infected the girl by biting her. And that fear had caused Tommy to rush the girl to their trysting place so they could check to see whether she had really been bitten; otherwise they would have continued to stroll leisurely and might well have stopped when the girl had said 'Look, a turtle' for a closer look. And a closer look would have shown them– well, from above they'd only have decided it was a species of turtle they hadn't seen before, but that might have led one of them to pick it up for a closer look. And that would have been bad, because they would then have seen that it wasn't a turtle at all. Instead of having a plastrum, or bottom shell, under the carapace, it was one continuous shell with no openings for head or feet. They, or someone they took it to, might all too well have decided to crack it open to see what was inside. And that would have been all for the mind thing; even if it had found itself a host meanwhile it would have died in its host as well as in its own body. The mental extension of itself that controlled a host could not have independent existence.

Now he made Tommy sprint until he was well out of sight from the path and then, having learned that he could not keep up that pace for the half mile to the cave, slowed him down to a jog trot.

The entrance to the cave was small; one had to get down on hands and knees to go through it and, the mind thing saw with satisfaction, it was well screened by bushes.

Inside it was dim but, even through Tommy's eyes, he could see. But through Tommy's memory as well as Tommy's eyes he had a full picture of the place. (His sense of perception, which was independent of light or dark, functioned only when he was, sans host, in his own body. When in a host he was dependent upon the host's sensory organs, whatever they might be.) The cave wasn't a large one; it went back about twenty feet, and at its widest place, near the centre, it was about six feet wide, and only at that point was it high enough for a man to stand erect.

At about that point the mind thing had Tommy put him down and then scrabble with his hands a hole in the sand. About nine inches down his/Tommy's hands found rock. He had Tommy put him down in the hole and then cover him and smooth the ground carefully. Then, on hands and knees, back to the entrance Tommy went, smoothing away as he backed the marks he had made coming in. The sand was as smooth now as when he had entered.

And he had Tommy sit just outside the cave entrance – but screened and hidden by the same bushes that hid the entrance itself – and wait.

Now there was no hurry. He was safely hidden now and he could take his time to digest all the knowledge that was in Tommy's mind, to catalogue it and, using it as a basis, to lay his own long-range plans.

And to lay short-range plans for his host. Already he knew

that Tommy's mind was not the one he needed, ultimately, to control. But Tommy would serve for a while. Tommy probably had an average – but no better than average – IQ for his race (at least that was the way Tommy thought of himself), but he was only partly educated and had no knowledge whatsoever of science beyond a very few and extremely elementary principles.

But Tommy could serve him – for a while.

CHAPTER THREE

Charlotte Garner awoke, as suddenly and completely as a kitten awakens, completely oriented even before she opened her eyes. Her naked body felt uncomfortably cool and she shivered a little and then, opening her eyes, saw why the coolness had wakened her. She'd gone to sleep in warm sunlight, now she was in shadow. That meant the sun was low in the west, down behind the thick bushes at that end of the open space. Startled, she held up her wrist watch to read it – and was even more startled. They'd slept three full hours. Even leaving this minute and walking fast, they'd be half an hour late at their respective homes for dinner. Probably their folks, or hers anyway, were beginning to worry a little already.

Quickly she turned over to waken Tommy. Tommy wasn't there. But his clothes were there, just past where he'd been lying. After a brief shock, she realised what had happened, the only thing that could have happened. Tommy must have wakened a minute or so before she had, and before dressing himself or wakening her, he had gone out of the clearing somewhere nearby to answer a call of nature. He wouldn't have, couldn't have, gone any farther than that, for that or for any other reason, without his clothes. He'd be back in a minute.

And since he didn't carry or wear a watch he probably didn't realise quite how late it was. But *she* did. She stood up and brushed off the little grass that stuck to her body and then dressed quickly; there were only four garments – panties, bra, skirt, and sweater – and it didn't take her long to get them on. Then she sat down and strapped on the barefoot sandals, and stood up again.

Still no sign of Tommy; and while she wasn't worried yet, she wanted him to hurry, so she called out his name, but there wasn't any answer. He'd hardly have gone out of hearing distance – but probably he was already on his way back and for that reason hadn't bothered to answer. She realised that there was likely some grass in her hair, so she went to Tommy's clothes and got out the little pocket comb he kept clipped in his shirt pocket, ran it a few times through her short bobbed hair, and put it back.

Still no Tommy, and now she was getting a little worried. Not that she could think of anything that could have happened to him. She called out his name again, much more loudly this time, and then, 'Answer me. Where are you?'

She listened hard, but there was only the faint rustle of leaves in a breeze that had just sprung up. Could Tommy be trying to frighten her? No, he wouldn't do anything like that.

But what could have happened? He couldn't have *gone* anywhere, naked except for those bright blue short socks he hadn't taken off. Could he have fainted, or had an accident? Fainting seemed impossible; Tommy was in perfect health. And if an accident – well, it would have to be the kind of accident that would make him unconscious (she didn't dare think the word *dead*). If he'd just turned an ankle or even broken a leg, he'd still have answered her. In fact, he'd have wakened her sooner by calling her. She was a light sleeper and would have heard him call her from any reasonable distance.

Really worried now, she went out of the clearing through the bushes and started to circle around it, looking everywhere, behind bushes and trees, even on the side towards the path, although he surely wouldn't have gone that way; not for the purpose she'd originally thought of as his only reason for leaving her at all – and she still couldn't think of any other.

From time to time she called his name, and she was shouting now. She spiralled out, and when she realised, half an hour later, that she was a hundred yards or so from her starting point and had thoroughly searched an area with a hundred-yard radius, she was really scared. He wouldn't possibly have come this far.

She needed help, she realised. She hurried back to the path and started home, half walking, half running, keeping the fastest pace she thought she might possibly maintain for three miles. She'd have to tell them the truth, she realised, no matter what they thought about, or did about, Tommy and her jumping the gun and having premarital relations. No holding that back, since Tommy's clothes would have to be the starting point of the search. But that didn't matter now. Only finding Tommy mattered.

She was a tired, panting, dishevelled girl when she stumbled into her parents' living-room. They were listening to the radio but her father turned it off quickly and glared at her. 'Fine time! I was just about to—' Then he saw her face and said, 'What's wrong, Charl?'

She blurted it out. She was interrupted only once, by her mother's shocked voice. 'You mean you and Tommy have been—' But her father stopped that. 'Worry about that later, Mom. Let her finish.'

Jed Garner stood up. 'I'll call Gus,' he said. 'We'll get out there right away. He can bring Buck.'

He went to the phone and called Gus Hoffman, who lived on the next farm, and started talking.

On the other end of the line, Gus Hoffman listened grimly. All he said when Garner had finished was, 'Be right there.'

He hung up the phone and stood a moment thinking. Then he went to a hamper of dirty clothes and found a sock of Tommy's, put it in his pocket. He'd want it to get Buck started on Tommy's trail. Not that Buck didn't already know Tommy's scent, but he wouldn't know he was supposed to follow it unless there was something of Tommy's to hold in front of his nose while you said, 'Find 'im, boy.'

He got Buck's leash from its nail in the kitchen and put it in another pocket. Buck was a good dog on a trail but he had one fault. Once you started him tracking you had to put him on a leash and keep him on it. Otherwise, since at least part of the time he wouldn't call back, he could get so far ahead you could lose him. Even following a trail, if it's a fresh and hot one, a dog can sometimes go faster than a man can keep up with him.

He made sure that he had matches, got the lantern and checked that it was full, then went out of the kitchen door.

Buck was sleeping not in but in front of the doghouse Tommy had built for him. Buck was a big liver-and-white-coloured dog; he wasn't all one breed, but he was all hound. He was seven years old, past his prime but still with a few good years in him.

'Come on, Buck,' Hoffman said, and the dog fell in behind him as he went around the house and cut across the fields to the Garner farmhouse. It was just dusk.

They'd seen him coming and came outside, the three of them. Jed Garner had a lantern too, and a shotgun under his other arm.

There weren't any greetings. Hoffman asked Charlotte, 'This path, it's the one that turns off the road to the north just past the bridge?'

'Yes, Mr Hoffman. But I'm going along. I'll have to go to show you the place where we – where we went. Where his clothes are.'

'You're *not* going, Charl,' her father said firmly. 'If for no other reason than that you're already so exhausted from practically running back the three miles, that you'd slow us down.'

'Buck will take us to the clothes,' Hoffman said. 'Then we'll have him circle the spot and pick up the trail. You said three miles – and it's about one to where the path starts. That'd make it about two miles back into the woods. Right?'

Charlotte nodded.

'Let's get going then,' Hoffman said to Garner.

'Wait, Gus. Why don't we take my car for the first mile along the road? Save time.'

'You forget about Buck,' Hoffman said. 'He ain't gun-shy, but he's car-shy. If we force him into a car he'd keep trying to jump out, and anyway it'd make him so damn nervous he might not be any good to us. We'll have to walk. Come on.'

The two men went out to the road and started along it. There was a bright moon; they weren't going to need the lanterns until they were in among trees. And it wasn't fully dark yet, anyway.

'Why the gun, Jed?' Hoffman asked. 'Thinking of a shotgun wedding?'

'Hell, no. Just that in the woods at night I feel better with one. Even though I know nothing's likely to jump me.' After a minute he added, 'I was just thinking, though. If we find Tommy—'

'We'll find him.'

'All right, *after* we find him. If he's all right, I don't think we ought to make those kids wait another six months. If they're playing house anyway, what the hell, let 'em make it legal. And you wouldn't want your first grandchild born too soon after the wedding, would you? I wouldn't.'

'All right,' Hoffman said.

They walked in silence for a while. Then they saw the headlights of a car coming towards them on the road and Hoffman turned quickly and got a grip on Buck's collar, and pulled him off the side of the road. 'Wait till it's by,' he said to Garner. 'Don't want Buck to bolt, and he might.'

After the car was past them, they started walking again.

By the time they reached the start of the path it was fully dark except for the moonlight and they stopped and lighted their lanterns. From here on, part of the time they'd be under trees and need light.

They walked on. Garner asked, 'Where the hell *could* Tommy have headed for, taking off stark naked that way?'

Hoffman grunted. 'Let's not wonder. Let's find out.'

Again they walked in silence until Hoffman said, 'I figure we've come about a mile since the road. How about you?'

'I guess about that,' Garner said. 'Maybe a mite over.'

'Then we better let Buck take over. Your gal could be wrong about the distance, and we don't want to overshoot.'

He put down his lantern and snapped the leash on to Buck's collar, then held Tommy's dirty sock to Buck's nose, 'Find 'im, boy.'

The dog sniffed the path and started off at once. They followed, Hoffman holding the leash in one hand and the lantern in the other, Garner bringing up the rear. Buck kept moving steadily but not too fast for them; there was no strain on the leash.

About a mile farther on (Charlotte's judgement of the distance had been just about right) Buck wandered slightly off the path and sniffed something.

Hoffman bent over to look. 'Dead field mouse. Squashed. Come on, Buck, back to business.' He pulled Buck back to the path.

Garner said, 'Charl told me about that – while we were waiting for you to come over. Didn't seem important, so I didn't mention it. But it means we're right close to the place. I mean to the place where they – went to sleep.'

'What did she tell you about a field mouse?'

Garner told him. And then said, 'Damn funny thing, a

field mouse acting like that. Say, what if the thing *was* rabid? It didn't bite Charl, didn't break her skin, I mean; but Tommy brushed it off his pants leg. What if his finger hit its teeth and one of 'em broke the skin a little without his realising it, would that account for—?'

'Hell, Jed, you know better than that about rabies. If Tommy was infected, it wouldn't affect him this soon, or that way. It takes days.' Hoffman rubbed his chin. 'Just the same, when we find Tommy I'm going to check his hands. If there's even a scratch, we'll pick up that mouse on our way back, and have it checked. Come on, Buck, get going again.'

Only about thirty paces farther on Buck turned off the path again and this time he didn't stop to sniff anything. He kept going. He led them back to where some clumps of bushes made a solid wall and started to push his way through them. Hoffman parted the bushes and held his lantern forward.

'This is it,' he said. 'His clothes are still here.' He stepped through and Garner followed. They stood looking down.

'God damn,' Hoffman said. 'I'd hoped—' He didn't finish the sentence. He'd hoped the clothes would be gone, that Tommy would have returned here after Charlotte had left. He didn't know what that would have meant – since Tommy hadn't come home – but it seemed less dangerous than the alternative, Tommy being out there somewhere and still naked, whatever else might have happened to him. At any rate, he was more frightened now than when he had first heard the girl's story. The clothes looked so – empty. Until now this had seemed like a bad dream; it was becoming a nightmare.

Buck was sniffing eagerly at the clothes and then at the grass where Tommy had lain. Then, circling, he started for the bushes, at a different point this time.

Hoffman let him through and went through behind him.

'Come on, Jed,' he said. 'He's got the trail again, the way Tommy left.'

Garner said, 'Shall I bring the clothes?'

Hoffman hesitated. 'All right,' he said. 'When we find him, he'll need 'em and no use our having to come back.'

He waited, holding Buck back, until Garner had made a bundle of the clothes and rejoined him with them.

Then he started following the pull of the leash. Back to the path first and then off it at a diagonal, towards the north-west.

Buck was straining hard at the leash now. Not only was the trail fresher, but a man wearing only socks leaves a stronger scent than one wearing shoes. Also, on the path, there had been other if fainter human scents. Now there were none.

'Easy, boy,' Hoffman said, as he and Garner followed the straining dog.

CHAPTER FOUR

The mind thing rested now. He had neatly catalogued and indexed, mentally, everything in the mind of his present host.

He knew everything about this planet Earth that Tommy knew, which was enough to give him a rough overall picture. He knew its approximate size, although not in figures, and he knew that it was mostly salt water but had considerable land area too, in several continents. He knew roughly how the world was divided into countries and the names and approximate locations and sizes of the most important of those countries.

His knowledge of local terrain and geography was much better. He knew that he was in wild country, hunting country, but only about four miles north of the nearest town. Its name was Bartlesville, and it had about two thousand inhabitants. It was in a state called Wisconsin, which was a part of a country called the United States of America. The nearest large town, or small city, about forty-five miles to the south-east, was Green Bay. Something over a hundred miles south of Green Bay was Milwaukee, the nearest large city. And ninety miles or so south of Milwaukee was a much larger city, one of the largest, Chicago. He could visualise those places; Tommy had been to them. But no farther; Chicago was as far from home as Tommy had been. But Bartlesville and the country around it he knew very well. And that was good, for this area might have to be the mind thing's scene of operations for some time. In addition to its geography, he now knew its flora and fauna. The flora didn't interest him, but the fauna did. He had mental pictures now of all the creatures of the countryside, wild and domestic. And he knew their abilities and limitations. If he should have to use an animal host again he would know which to choose for the job at hand.

Most important, he knew that man was the only intelligent species on Earth, and that man had science, apparently a fairly advanced science. While Tommy's knowledge of science was almost nil (he knew a little about elementary electricity, enough to wire a doorbell), he knew that science and scientists existed, and that (this was of major importance) science included electronics. The meaning of the word electronics was vague to him, but he had seen (and owned) a radio set. He had seen television. And he knew what radar did, if not how it worked. Where these things existed there was knowledge of electronics.

And the mind thing's eventual goal was to obtain control of an electronicist, one who not only knew the subject but who had or could obtain access to equipment and components. It would probably take him several steps – several intervening hosts – to get there, but he knew now that it could be done if he planned properly. And he had to do it. He wanted to go home.

He came from a planet of a sun seventy-three light-years away, in the direction of the constellation Andromeda, a sun too faint from Earth ever to have been named, although it has a number in Earth's star catalogues.

He had not come voluntarily; he had been sent. Not as a scout or as the spearhead of an invasion (although it could turn out that way if he could get back), but as an exile. He was a criminal. To explain what his crime had been would require the explanation of a social system so utterly alien to ours as to be almost incomprehensible; suffice it to say that he had committed a crime and that his punishment was exile.

He had not come in a spaceship. He had been sent along a – call it a force beam; that's a poor description of it but is as nearly accurate as any other simple phrase, in our language, would be. Transmission had been instantaneous; one second he was in the projector back home, the next second he was lying beside a path in the woods north of Bartlesville, Wisconsin, having experienced no impact on arrival.

The planet of his exile had been chosen at random, and with no knowledge of whether it was inhabited or inhabitable, out of the billions of planets in the galaxy which his race had charted but had never got around to investigating; there were so many billion planets that they never would get around to investigating more than a small fraction of them. The reason why they were able to chart planets as readily as we chart stars was that their equivalent of a telescope, based on magnification of the sense of perception instead of the far inferior sense of sight, enabled them to 'see' planets almost as far as we are able to see stars.

So now he was here, and now he wanted to go home. It was far from impossible, for two reasons.

First, he had been extremely lucky in having come to a planet that had not only reasonably intelligent beings, but a science and a technology, however inferior to his own. The chances had been, say, a hundred thousand to one against it. If he had been sent to an uninhabited planet, he would have been completely helpless. If to a planet that had life but had not yet developed intelligence (like Earth of a million years ago) he *might* have been able to construct a projector to send himself back but the odds were against it. (Can you imagine the difficulties of a dinosaur, even with intelligent direction, in finding and refining germanium and then using it to make a transistor?)

Second, he would be welcomed home and pardoned –

even honoured – if he could get there. The exiles always had that chance, and one out of hundreds of them made it.

A returned exile was honoured very highly indeed, and became a hero, if he brought back with him news of a species better fitted for hosts than the ones in current use. And that the mind thing could do. In having Tommy carry him he had discovered the opposable thumb and it was, as far as he knew, unique in the galaxy. It made grasping and handling things so much easier. Quite possibly he could make his projector big enough to let him take a sample human host back with him. If he did that he would save them sending a scouting expedition; they could make their first slave raid in full force.

All that was within his grasp if he worked slowly and carefully and made no mistakes. He had made one already, he now realised. He had lessened his present host's value to him by making him act in a manner against human mores, thereby attracting attention to him. For a while at least Tommy Hoffman would be an object of curiosity and suspicion, which would somewhat limit his usefulness. People would be watching him to see if he did anything *else* that seemed strange to them.

What he should have done, and would have done if he had taken a few minutes to study Tommy's thoughts, was this: He should have had Tommy come to him and move him from his dangerously exposed position, but not all the way to the cave. Tommy could have moved him to a place of temporary concealment – the high grass only a few feet off the path would have been good enough – and then returned and lain down beside the sleeping girl and pretended to sleep himself. That would have given him time to learn enough about Tommy and the girl, about human actions and emotions, so that when they awakened, he could have appeared to her to be perfectly normal. Possibly he could even (again to use the euphemistic phrase from Tommy's mind) have 'gone another round' with her. The mind thing wouldn't have enjoyed it, of course; when in a host he felt no pain when he had it killed, but neither did he share any of its pleasurable sensations. He would have had intercourse with the girl simply because it would have been the natural thing for Tommy to have done.

Then they would have dressed and returned home as they had intended to do. (Once inside a host, he could control it at any reasonable distance.) In the morning Tommy could have come back, alone, and moved him to this much better place of concealment in the cave, and then returned home without having aroused anyone's curiosity.

That's what he should have done, but it was too late by the time he realised it. His alternate plan would have to suffice. It was based on the concept of something called amnesia that he had found in Tommy's mind.

Tommy could stay here on guard in front of the cave entrance all night. Early in the morning he could go back and get his clothes (the girl would have left when she got worried enough, but she wouldn't have taken them) and walk home. His story would be simple. He and the girl had got tired and lain down to rest. He'd gone to sleep. And at dawn he'd wakened up in a different place over a mile away and with no recollection of how he got there. He could hardly have walked that far in his sleep – and besides Tommy had never sleep-walked – so he must have had some reason for going there, but he couldn't remember what it was. It must be amnesia. They'd have him talk to a doctor a time or two, but nothing would come of that. And henceforth Tommy would at least in the sight of others appear to act completely normal – until his usefulness as a host came to an end; then he would either kill himself or, if possible, arrange his own death in some manner that would make it seem accidental.

Besides its simplicity and incontrovertibility, Tommy's

story had another advantage, it would not cross up the girl's story whichever way she told it. She might have been frightened enough to tell her family the whole truth – that she and Tommy had slept naked and that he had gone off in that state, or she might well have left that part out. If his first story didn't mention clothes at all and if she hadn't, then their stories would match. If taxed with the fact that she had told the story differently, he could sheepishly admit that, yes, he had been naked when he had gone to sleep and had awakened the same way in the morning. His original omission of that part of the story would be entirely understandable to everyone.

Short- and long-range planning were suddenly interrupted. Through Tommy's eyes peering through the bushes that masked the cave entrance, the mind thing saw two bobbing lights coming; through Tommy's ears it heard the excited baying of a hound on a scent, and recognised the dog's voice as that of Buck, Tommy's father's dog.

Immediately he realised what had happened. Tommy's father had been much more worried than Tommy could have realised. (Probably Charlotte had told the whole truth – Tommy's leaving her without his clothes would have been more puzzling and frightening than if he had wandered off clothed.) And Tommy had thought (or rather, Tommy's mind would have thought if Tommy himself had been the one using it) that they might come to look for him tomorrow but not tonight, after dark. Tommy's mind simply hadn't thought at all of the possibility of Buck's being used to track him down.

But now they were coming, two men and the dog. One of the men would be Tommy's father, the other probably Charlotte's father.

And the dog would lead them straight to the cave!

He had to distract them, lead them away. Even if it cost him his present host, he couldn't let attention be drawn to the cave. They were less than a hundred yards away and were heading straight for it, the dog following Tommy's trail.

Tommy, or Tommy's body, jumped up and ran around the bushes and towards the approaching lanterns. He ran until he was within the circle of light of the first one and then stopped. Buck barked joyously and strained at the leash to run to him. Gus Hoffman shouted, 'Tommy! What the hell—?'

Too near the cave. He turned and started to run again, diagonally away from the cave. He heard them start after him, still calling. 'Tommy! Tommy, stop!' He heard Garner say, 'Slip the dog's leash. Buck can catch him.' And his father's reply, 'Sure, and run *with* him. We'd just lose both of them.'

He couldn't run in a straight line because he had to keep to open areas where the moonlight would let him see. Occasionally, while they were still close enough to follow him by sight, they could take short cuts through shadow because of their lanterns, but he could run much faster and was soon outdistancing them. Then he was definitely out of their sight and knew they'd have to let Buck do the trailing again and follow his roundabout course; that would slow them down still more.

He was able to rest a moment then, to catch his breath, and when he started again it was at a fast trot instead of a sprint. He knew where he was going now, and he began to circle to take himself back to his starting point.

And from there to the place, only a very short distance away, where he had perceived the artifact (he knew now what it was, a jack-knife) before the two humans had come along the path.

It was in deep grass, and in shadow. Tommy's sense of sight didn't help at all now, and he had to have Tommy's hands grope and feel. It was awkward, but he knew where it was, within inches, and finally Tommy's fingers closed over it and picked it up.

He broke one of Tommy's thumbails trying to open the full-length rusted blade, but finally he got it open with the other nail.

Without hesitation Tommy slashed one of his wrists, changed the knife to his other hand, and slashed the other wrist. Both cuts were deep, almost to the bone, and blood spurted freely. He didn't lie down, but within a minute loss of blood blacked him out and he fell heavily.

He was dead when the two men and the dog reached him.

And the mind of the mind thing was safely back within itself, buried under nine inches of sand in the cave.

CHAPTER FIVE

It had been a bad night for Gus Hoffman.

He had waited with the body while Jed Garner had gone back for help. While he waited he dressed Tommy's body in the clothes Garner had been carrying. Not because he had any intention of lying to the sheriff about how they had found Tommy, but because it just didn't seem decent for the body to be taken in naked.

Garner went straight home. After reaching the road he passed three other farms before he came to his own, but he wanted Charlotte to be the first to know and didn't want to tell her over a phone. She took the news more quietly than he had dared to hope, mostly because she was ready for it; she had felt instinctively from the moment she'd had to start home alone that she'd never see Tommy alive again.

Then Garner phoned the sheriff at Wilcox, the county seat, twenty miles away. The sheriff came in an ambulance to carry the body into town and, so the body could be examined quickly, he brought the coroner with him. Garner took them to the spot, and the four men, taking turns, carried Tommy out of the woods on a stretcher. Buck stayed with the party until the engine of the ambulance started: then he bolted home across the fields.

At the mortuary in Bartlesville the coroner examined the body while the sheriff talked to Hoffman and Garner. The coroner joined them to report that there was no doubt about the cause of death – loss of blood from the slashed wrists – and that the only other marks on the body were briar scratches on the legs and cuts and bruises on the bottoms of the feet. He was willing to do an autopsy if the sheriff requested it but said he didn't see what an autopsy could possibly bring out that wasn't already obvious.

The sheriff had gone along with that, but he said he thought an inquest should be held. There'd be no doubt about the verdict, suicide while of unsound mind, but he hoped something might be brought out that would help clear up the mystery of the reason for sudden and violent insanity in a boy who had never shown the slightest symptom even of instability. Also there was a minor mystery in the suicide weapon, the rusty, broken pocket knife. Hoffman was positive that it had never been Tommy's. And both Hoffman and Garner swore that when they had seen Tommy briefly before he ran away from them he could not possibly have been carrying anything; his hands had been open at his sides. He must have picked up the knife where he had used it, but how could he have known it was there, or found it in the dark?

'All right,' the sheriff said, 'we'll set the inquest for two o'clock tomorrow afternoon. That okay with everybody?'

Hoffman and Garner nodded, but the coroner asked, 'Why so soon, Hank?'

'Had this in mind, Doc. Something just might come out at the inquest that might change our minds about an autopsy. Of course if there is an autopsy, the sooner the better. We'll have the inquest right here at the mortuary, good a place as any here, and there's no use moving it over to Wilcox. And, Gus, right after the inquest you can go ahead and make funeral arrangements. As soon as convenient if there's not going to be an autopsy – and I doubt if there will be. Who was Tommy's doctor? Doc Gruen?'

'Yeah,' Hoffman said. 'Not that Tommy saw him often. He was pretty healthy.'

'We'll put him on the stand anyway. And maybe some of Tommy's teachers – but I'll check with them first, see if they ever noticed anything unusual that ought to go in the record. No use calling them if they haven't.'

He turned to Garner. 'Uh – Jed. Charlotte'll have to testify. I'll go as easy on her as I can, but it'll have to be brought out that Tommy was naked when he went off. To show he was – uh – off his rocker even then and didn't leave her for any sane reason like being mad at her, and then go off his rocker after. But what I'm getting at is – I can clear the court, except for the coroner's jury, while we take her testimony. Want me to?'

Garner scratched his head and thought a minute. He said, 'I guess not, Sheriff. I think I can answer for her that she'd just as soon testify in front of everybody. Hell, the whole story's going to get out anyway and maybe sound worse, and like we're ashamed of her. Damn it, what they did wasn't so bad – they were in love and engaged, just jumped the gun a little. Don't tell my wife I told you this, but she and I did the same thing, so how can we bawl out Charlotte? And if the town or the neighbours turn thumbs down on her for it, the hell with 'em. I'll sell the farm and move. Always kind of wanted to go to California anyway.'

So things had been left. Gus Hoffman had got home by one o'clock, home to the loneliest, emptiest house he'd ever known. He'd thought he wouldn't be able to sleep, until he remembered that there was most of a pint of medicinal whisky in the cupboard. He got it, and a glass. He wasn't a drinking man; he took an occasional nip on special occasions to be sociable, but this was more whisky than he ordinarily drank in the course of a year. Tonight, though, if this was enough whisky to bring oblivion, he was willing to let it. Tonight was the worst night of his life, even worse than the night his wife had died. For one thing, he'd known for weeks that she was dying; he'd been prepared for it. For another, he'd still had Tommy. Tommy had been three then, but Gus had managed to keep him on the farm and raise him there, with the help, until Tommy was of school age, of a woman who came daily to take care of him while Gus worked the farm.

Now he was completely alone, permanently alone. He knew that he'd never marry again. Not because he was too old – he was still a year short of fifty – but because never since his wife's death had he ever even thought about living with another woman, or wanting one. He didn't know why it was impossible for him, but it was. Something in him had died when his wife had died. It was something psychological, of course, but it was something more than psychological impotence. A man suffering from that can still *want* a woman, at least in the abstract, and freeze only when he tries to have one in the flesh. But Gus Hoffman couldn't even want one; nor could he entertain the thought of making a sexless marriage just to have a woman around the house for companionship and as a helpmate. He didn't want a woman around the house, even on that basis. (Having Charlotte around as Tommy's wife would have been different, of course; he'd looked forward to that.)

All his hopes had been in Tommy. He was not a demonstrative man and had never let Tommy know how important to him had been the boy's decision to stay on the farm with him, even after his marriage. He'd wanted grandchildren and now he'd never have them; he was now the last of his line, a dead end.

Unless— With his third drink a sudden blazing hope came to him. Unless he was already scheduled to have a grandson. Charlotte could be pregnant and not even know it yet. Or had Tommy taken precautions against that happening?

Suddenly he wanted to know right away. He got up from

the kitchen table to go to the telephone. Then he sat down again, realising he shouldn't call the Garners in the middle of the night to ask them that. In fact, he shouldn't ask them at all. He should wait and see, and keep his hope alive for as long as he could.

Meanwhile it would give him something to think about besides his grief and loneliness. He could even plan. If and when Garner learned that Charlotte was pregnant he'd surely sell out and move away; he'd said he'd do that anyway if he found Charlotte in disgrace in the town or neighbourhood – and while an affair might be forgiven her, an illegitimate child certainly wouldn't. Well, Gus Hoffman would sell out too and go with them, wherever they went, California or the moon. If possible, he'd talk Garner into their buying a farm together so he could live with them – or make himself living quarters in the barn if they didn't want him underfoot in the house – and help raise his grandson. Or granddaughter; he'd even settle for that. If Jed wouldn't agree to buying a farm jointly, he'd buy his as near as possible. The next-door one if he could get it, even if he had to pay a premium price to talk someone into selling it. Price need be no object, thank God; he had twelve thousand dollars in the bank and investments, besides what he'd get for his farm here. And he'd had some pretty good offers for that.

He finished the whisky and realised that for almost the first time in his life, certainly for the first time since his twenties, he was drunk. When he stood up he found he had to hold on to things to keep from falling. He didn't bother to go upstairs or to undress; he made his way as far as the living-room sofa. He managed to get his shoes off, and that was the last he remembered.

That had been last night.

And now it was morning. He'd wakened at dawn. He'd made coffee and forced himself to eat some oatmeal. He'd done his milking and put out the cans for the dairy's route man to pick up, and had done the few other things that had to be done. All that took two hours, and it was still early. There was still work – there's always work to do on a farm – but nothing that couldn't wait until late afternoon, after the inquest. And he'd thought of something more important than work that he wanted to do.

He felt to make sure that Buck's leash and Tommy's sock were still in his pocket from last night, and then called Buck and walked across the fields to Jed Garner's farm.

Garner was hoeing in a small garden patch behind the house. He stopped and leaned on his hoe as Hoffman came up.

'Morning,' Hoffman said. 'How's Charlotte?'

'Still asleep, I hope. Didn't get to sleep till God knows when last night. What's on your mind, Gus?'

'Just dropped by to tell you where I'm heading. Back to where – where we were last night.'

'Why?'

'Just want a look around by daylight. The place where we found Tommy's clothes, the place where we found *him*. We might've missed something, just with lanterns. I don't know what, but if there's anything to find now's the time, before the inquest.'

'Makes sense,' Garner said.

'Another thing, why I'm taking Buck. I'm going to where we first saw Tommy, when he ran up to us. See if Buck can back-trail him from there, find out where he'd been, in that direction. Dunno it'll tell me anything, but I want to know.'

'I'll go with you,' Garner said. 'Might as well. Don't feel like working and I guess you're the same way. Wait till I tell Maw.'

Gus Hoffman waited for him, and the two men started off.

The mind thing wasn't worried, but he was annoyed with

himself for having panicked and killed his first, and thus far only, human host. Subsequent and calmer thought showed him that it hadn't been necessary. He had to lead them away from the cave, yes, but after that there had been no need for him to make his host kill himself. After he'd led them a safe distance he could have fallen and pretended to be asleep or unconscious when they reached him. When they awakened him he could have been surprised to find himself there, especially to find himself naked, and he could have remembered nothing since going to sleep beside his girl at their trysting place. True, his case would not have been diagnosed as simply amnesia, not after running away from his father as he had, but it would still have been called only temporary insanity. They wouldn't have locked him up in an asylum for that, which had been the thought that had made him make Tommy destroy himself – incarcerated, he would have been completely valueless as a host; also, he knew from Tommy's mind that mental institutions take elaborate precautions to prevent their inmates from committing suicide, and he might have been stuck in Tommy's mind for quite a while. And an unsuccessful attempt at suicide might have got him into a padded cell, which would have made it impossible.

But he realised now that they would not have incarcerated Tommy, not for one brief period of temporary insanity. They'd have watched him for a while, but not too closely or for too long, if he seemed again perfectly normal. There'd have been a talk with the doctor, of course, and he would probably have recommended taking Tommy to a specialist, a psychiatrist. But that would be good because, since there were no psychiatrists in Bartlesville or even in Wilcox (that Tommy had known of), it would have meant a trip to Green Bay or possibly even to Milwaukee. Either of those places would have a public library large enough to be worth while for him, and if he could have had some free time – or even have made a getaway for a while, if accompanied – he could have made at least a good start on learning some of the things he would have to know.

Yes, as Tommy's mind would have expressed it, he had goofed. However, he couldn't blame himself too much. It is tremendously difficult to understand immediately all the ins and outs of a completely alien world, a completely alien culture. Especially since thus far his only concepts of that world, beyond his immediate range of perception, had come from the mind of a not too bright, not too well educated high school boy who had taken no interest in any serious subject except farming. Tommy would have made an excellent farmer.

The main disadvantage of his present position, safe though he thought it was, was the fact that from here it would be almost impossible to get another human host. Men came through these woods, usually to hunt, but the chances of one happening to go to sleep near enough, within the forty-yard extreme range of his perceptive sense, were remote.

To get his next human host he'd have to use an animal host first, to transport him near enough to a place where a human would be sleeping. There would be risk in that, during transport, but it was a risk he would have to take. And, although he had actually not encountered as yet any animals within his range, he'd learned from Tommy that there were such animals, several of them. A deer could carry him easily in its mouth; so could a bear. There might be air transport, too. A chicken hawk, since it could carry off a chicken heavier than he was, would be ideal. An owl might serve; Tommy had known that owls swoop down on mice and fly with them, but he'd had no clear idea of how heavy an object an owl could fly with.

On the whole, he thought, a bird would be best. A deer or a bear might have trouble with fences, and if there was a dog in the farmyard it would bark and waken the household. But a dog would not notice a chicken hawk circling down in the middle of the night to leave something on the roof. Then, as soon as the hawk had flown away and killed itself or got itself killed, he would have his choice of hosts among however many people would be sleeping in the house. The first act of his new host would be to retrieve the mind thing's corporeal self from its exposed position on the roof and put it in a safe place of concealment.

There was no hurry; this time he would think every detail through and make no more mistakes. Besides, no owl or chicken hawk had as yet come within his perception range. Nor a deer nor a bear. Only field mice, rabbits, and other small creatures had as yet passed within range.

But he had studied them, each of them. One can never tell when a small animal might, for some special purpose – burrowing under a wall, for instance – make a better host, temporarily, than a larger one.

Once he had studied an animal inside and out – studied it himself, not just examined the concept of it in a host's mind – he could get himself a host of that species at any distance up to about ten miles, provided that one was sleeping within that range. Having studied a rabbit, for instance, he had only to concentrate on the concept of a rabbit, if one was sleeping within ten miles or so – the nearest one, if there were several. Once a hawk had flown past within his range – no matter at how fast a speed – he'd be able to get himself a hawk for a host any time he wanted one, if it was during the night when hawks slept. Sooner or later hawk, owl, deer, bear would come within range; he'd have himself a wide variety of potential animal hosts.

Things would have been easy for him – there'd have been no problem at all to speak of – if the same thing could have been done to highly intelligent hosts – which in the case of this planet meant human beings. Such creatures automatically resisted being taken over, and there was always a mental struggle sometimes lasting for seconds. To win he had to use all his power and to have the creature, the individual creature, within the limit of his senses of perception. And, of course, asleep.

That had been found to be true on almost all the inhabited planets which his species had visited or occupied. But there were rare exceptions, and during the night he had experimented to make sure Earth was not one of them.

He tried a field mouse first, concentrating on one by using the one which had been his first terrestrial host as a prototype. Annoyingly, it took him almost an hour to kill it so he could get his mind back into himself. First he had tried running it head-on into a tree and then into a stone. But it was so light, had so little inertial mass, that even against the stone the impact had served only to stun it momentarily. It couldn't climb well enough, he discovered, to get sufficiently high into a tree for a fall to kill it. He had taken it into the open, into a patch of bright moonlight, and had run it in circles there, hoping that the movement would draw the attention of an owl or some other nocturnal predator. But no predator seemed to be around. Finally he did what he should have done in the first place: he examined its thoughts and memories, such as they were. And he learned that there was water nearby, a shallow brook. The field mouse had immediately run towards it and into the water, and drowned itself.

Then back in himself in the cave again, he made his second experiment. He knew that there would be men sleeping within a few miles, past the edge of the woods to the south. Within ten miles in that direction was the town of Bartlesville where hundreds of men would be asleep. Using Tommy as his prototype, he concentrated on *man*, any man asleep. Nothing happened.

He made one further experiment. With some intelligent species it was possible to take over one at a distance if, instead of concentrating on the species, one concentrated on an individual, one which had already been studied and memorised. After studying Tommy, but before entering him, he had studied the girl Charlotte, inside and out. He tried concentrating again. And again nothing happened.

Although he couldn't have known it, Charlotte wasn't asleep as yet; she had gone to bed but was still crying into her pillow. But that didn't matter because it wouldn't have worked if she had been sleeping; mankind was no exception to the general run of intelligent creatures in respect to the distance at which he could make one his host.

After that he had rested; not sleeping, for his species never slept, but postponing further active thinking and planning. In any case he would have to wait until he had had a chance to study more useful potential hosts than the rabbits, field mice, and other small creatures which were all that had thus far passed within his ken. No larger creature came that night.

But now he heard – felt the vibrations of – something large coming his way. Two somethings, he decided – then three. Two bipeds and a quadruped, but one much larger than a rabbit. He concentrated his perception to its utmost limit and within a minute or two they were within its range. It was the same trio that had come last night trailing Tommy – Tommy's father, Charlotte's father, and Buck, the dog, straining at the leash and heading straight for the cave. They were taking Tommy's back trail to see where he had been before he had run towards them.

But *why*? He had recognised the possibility of their doing so, but had discounted it, not seeing any reason why they would be interested in where Tommy had been, once he was dead. Besides, since Tommy he had had no host or potential host capable of defending him or moving him. Nothing bigger than a rabbit. The sudden thought came to him of finding a rabbit, if one was sleeping near enough, and having it run across the trail to distract the dog. But as quickly, he realised that it wouldn't work. The dog was on a leash and if he tried to run after a rabbit they'd hold him back and put him on the trail again.

He was completely helpless. If they found him there was nothing he could do about it, nothing at all. But he didn't panic because the chance that they would find him was slight. They'd have no reason for digging. They'd find the cave, of course, and enter it. They'd wonder why Tommy had come here – but they wouldn't dig, he felt almost sure.

Now Buck was leading them around the bushes into sight of the entrance. He paused briefly to sniff where Tommy had crouched behind the bushes, and then started into the cave. Hoffman pulled him back.

'Damn,' Garner said. 'A cave, he came to. Wish now we'd have brought a gun or two and a flashlight or two. Size of that entrance, it's just the kind of cave a bear might pick.'

Hoffman said, 'If Tommy was in there last night, there wasn't a bear there then. And a bear's more likely to be to home by night than by day.'

The mind thing understood, for it now knew the language that was being spoken. Before it had had a human host, such words would have been only meaningless sounds – like the sounds Tommy and the girl had made to each other along the path and in their hiding place before they had gone to sleep.

'Just the same, I'm going in,' Hoffman said.

'Just a minute, Gus. I'll go in with you. But we might as well be sensible. Take that leash off Buck's collar and let him go in first. If there *is* anything dangerous in there, he's got a hell of a lot better chance than either of us of getting out safe. He'll be on his feet and we'll be on hands and knees.'

'Guess that's sensible.' Hoffman unsnapped the leash from Buck's collar, and Buck darted into the cave. Halfway, as far as Tommy had gone, and that was the end of the trail. He lay down.

The men listened for a while. 'Guess it's all right,' Hoffman said. 'Nothing could have hurt him so fast he couldn't have let out a yip. I'm going in.'

He entered on his hands and knees, and Garner followed. When they reached the centre of the cave where Buck lay, they found the ceiling high enough and stood up. It was dim, but they could see a little.

'Well, this is it,' Garner said. 'Reckon this is as far in as he came, since Buck stopped here. And there's nothing here, but it's nice and cool. Let's sit down and rest a minute before we go back.'

They sat down. The mind thing studied the dog. It was his first chance to do so, and thus far this was the biggest potential animal host he had had a chance to study.

Henceforth, Buck might be his if he ever needed a dog. Or the nearest other dog that happened to be asleep.

And now Buck, relaxed from his tracking, went to sleep. The mind thing considered, but waited. In Buck, he would have only Buck's senses, not his own.

'I'm trying to figure why he came here,' Hoffman said.

'Anybody's guess, Gus. He was out of his mind, that's all. Probably discovered this cave when he was a kid and remembered it, came here to hide from – from whatever. You can't figure what's going through a guy's mind when he's out of his mind.'

'Could be, to hide. But what if he came here to hide *something*? Or dig up something he'd hid here before? Don't ask me what, but this is soft sand, easy digging even with your hands.'

'What would he be hiding? Or going to dig up?'

'Dunno. But if we found anything here—'

The struggle was less negligible than that with the mind of a field mouse, but the mind thing was in Buck's mind almost instantly. Buck lifted his head.

He – the mind thing in Buck – considered. He probably

couldn't kill both of these men, but he could manage with a sudden attack to get in bites on both of them before they could subdue or kill him. That would certainly distract them from digging, at least right away. Probably it would send them hurrying back to town and a doctor. If not because the bites themselves were bad enough, then because of the same fear of rabies that Tommy and the girl had felt.

Garner said, 'Not now, Gus. Look, I don't think we'll find anything or learn anything, but I'll go along on coming back with you and trying, tomorrow. Too dark in here, for one thing, to do a good job without flashlights or a lantern, and if we do it at all we might as well do a good job and be sure, huh? And it'll go quicker if we have a spade and a rake. Besides, there isn't time now. We won't get home much before lunch as it is, and after lunch we got to get cleaned up and dressed, for the inquest.'

'Guess you're right, Jed,' Gus said. 'Okay, we might as well take off now. Least, we learned one thing we can tell at the inquest. Where Tommy went. And where he must have stayed till he saw our lanterns coming. If he'd left the cave here when he saw our lanterns he'd have met us just about where he did.'

Buck put his head down again. When the men left to crawl out of the cave, he followed them, trotted alongside Hoffman as the real Buck would have done, for the two miles back to the road.

There he bolted suddenly away from them – along the road, but east, in the opposite direction from the way they were headed. He did not go back into the woods towards the cave; he didn't want them remotely to suspect that he might be going back there. Hoffman called after him, but he paid no attention and kept running.

When he was out of sight around a bend, he dropped to a trot and cut into the woods. There was no path here but, without regard to Buck's senses or his knowledge of the terrain, the mind thing had perfect orientation; he went straight back to the cave.

Once inside, Buck dug through nine inches of sand and picked up the mind thing's shell in his mouth, carried it out of the cave, and put it down gently. Then he went back into the cave and filled in the hole he had dug. When it was filled he rolled over it several times to eliminate all signs that there had ever been a hole there. Then he went outside and picked up the mind thing again in his mouth. It was no heavier than a partridge, and he was as soft-mouthed as he would have been in carrying a wounded bird.

He trotted into the woods, avoiding paths or even game trails, looking for the wildest, most secluded spot. In thick, high grass, screened by bushes, he found a small hollow log. It would serve, at least for a while. With his mouth he placed the mind thing in one end of the hollow log and with a paw pushed it in farther, completely out of sight.

Then he trotted on in the same direction – so that if anyone with another dog should follow Buck's trail, he'd simply be led past the log – and a hundred yards away sat down while the mind thing considered.

He was safe now from being found when the men came back to the cave to dig. But did he want to keep Buck as a host for a while? He considered carefully and decided against it. Buck had served his purpose, and if he stayed in Buck he would have only Buck's senses; he could not study other potential hosts and ready himself for them. He wanted to be able to get, when he wanted one, a hawk, an owl, a deer, other animals. And while he was in Buck he could not so ready himself by studying other creatures as they passed near him.

Buck trotted ahead, veering slowly till he was heading back towards the road.

At the edge of the road he waited until a car came along. Then, at the last moment, and before the driver could have time even to touch the brakes, he dashed forward, right under its wheels.

Back in himself in the hollow log one minute later (it had taken Buck just that long to die), the mind thing thought back over everything he had just done and decided that he had made no mistake this time.

Nor had he, except for one he could not possibly have foreseen. He should have let Buck wait for another car. The driver of the car that had killed Buck was Ralph S. Staunton, PhD, ScD, professor of physics at Massachusetts Institute of Technology.

Doc Staunton did not look impressive. He was small, about five feet six, and weighed slightly under a hundred and twenty-five pounds. He was fifty, and his crew-cut hair was greying, but he had a wiry strength and an agile body and mind that made him seem younger. The first thing you'd have noticed about him was his eyes, because they were the youngest thing about him. When he was amused, which was often, they didn't just twinkle; they seemed to sparkle like grey diamonds.

Right now, on vacation, he was dressed comfortably and somewhat sloppily, and he was in need of a shave. You'd never have guessed him to be one of the most brilliant men in the country.

CHAPTER SIX

Swearing under his breath, Doc Staunton braked the car to a stop. It hadn't been his fault; there was no possible way he could have avoided running over that dog, but still it was an unpleasant thing to have happened. What had been wrong with the dog? Mad and running blindly? It had simply come from nowhere, out of the bushes along the side of the road. Even if it hadn't stopped to look for cars, it couldn't have failed to *hear* his – the only sound in a quiet countryside. The car was a station wagon, ancient and quite noisy, that he had bought two weeks before in Green Bay after having flown that far. He'd paid so little for it that if he sold it even for junk at the end of this Wisconsin vacation it would have cost him less to own it than to have rented a car for six weeks.

He turned off the ignition, got out of the car and walked back, hoping that the dog was dead. It couldn't possibly survive; both the left front and the left rear wheels had gone squarely over its body. Since it would die anyway he hated the thought that it might have to live and suffer a while first. It was about twenty paces back from the car; it had taken him that far to stop. It didn't seem to be moving, nor was it making any sound that he could hear, but when he was about halfway to it he saw that it was still alive; its side moved with convulsive breathing.

Doc swore again and went back to the car. He didn't have

either of his guns in it, but a tyre iron would be better than nothing. He got one and hurried back to the dog, but it was dead by then; its eyes were open and glazed. Blood had run out of its mouth and there was no sign of breathing.

'Sorry, old boy,' Doc said softly. 'Guess I'll have to find out who owned you, and tell him.'

He bent down to lift the dog by its legs to move it off the edge of the road, but then he straightened up instead and stood thinking. The dog would have to be buried in any case, whether by him or by its owner, and it would be a much less pleasant job – because of ants and possibly buzzards – if he left it here while he did his errands in Bartlesville, which might take hours. He had no shovel in the station wagon but there was a tarpaulin which was old enough to be expendable. He got the tarpaulin and spread it out, folded once, on the road; then he lifted the dog on to it, rolled the tarpaulin around it a few times, and put it into the back of the station wagon.

In town a little later he made purchases at several different places, describing the dog – it had been a hound, male, liver and white – at each, and on the third try he found someone who said that it must be the dog that belonged to Gus Hoffman, and that Hoffman would be in town because he'd be attending the inquest on his son, who had committed suicide last night, that was being held at the local mortuary.

Doc Staunton had never attended an inquest and since he was mildly curious how one was run, he went to the mortuary and found it just starting. All the chairs were taken, but several other men were standing at the back of the room and Doc stood there too and listened.

Charlotte Garner was testifying, and Doc found himself increasingly fascinated. First by her calm and courageous frankness in telling the full truth about her relations with the boy Tommy Hoffman, and then by the story itself of how she had awakened to find Tommy's clothes, but not Tommy. When she'd finished describing searching and calling for him and then running home to tell her parents, the coroner tried to dismiss her, but there was, she said, one thing that she wanted to add; his questions had led her to skip the part about the field mouse and she wanted to put it in the testimony because she thought possibly it had bitten Tommy when it had tried to run up his leg and he had knocked it off with his hand. And that maybe he had been infected by some form of hydrophobia . . .

The coroner let her finish, but before calling his next witness he talked to the jury a moment, explaining the symptoms of hydrophobia and its relatively long incubation period; a bite from the mouse could not possibly have affected Tommy so suddenly nor, for that matter, in such a way. Besides, he said, while it was possible that the mouse had had hydrophobia, which would account for at least most of its actions, it had not bitten Tommy; the skin on his hands had been unbroken. There had been scratches on his legs, but these were caused by his running barelegged through bushes in the woods; none of the scratches could have been a bite.

Gus Hoffman testified next, then Jed Garner. Their stories were identical because they had been together all the time.

Doc Staunton listened carefully, especially when the dog Buck was mentioned – Buck following the boy last night, Buck leading them to the cave this morning. The sheriff testified last, about being called and going into the woods with Hoffman and Garner to bring out the body.

The coroner's jury went into another room but came back almost immediately with a verdict of suicide while temporarily insane. People began to wander off.

Doc started to make his way towards the man whom he now knew to be Gus Hoffman, owner of the dog, but Hoffman disappeared into an inner office of the mortuary, no doubt to discuss arrangements for the funeral, and Garner and Garner's daughter had gone with him.

Doc then cornered the big man who was the sheriff, introduced himself, and told about running over the dog.

'Maybe it's just as well, Sheriff,' he said, 'that I'm talking to you instead of Mr Hoffman because – well, Mr Hoffman had a nasty blow losing his son last night. Possibly it would be better if he doesn't learn right away that his dog is dead too. It might be kinder to let him think the dog has just run away or got lost, and to realise gradually that it won't be coming back. What do you think?'

The sheriff scratched his head. 'Well—' He hesitated.

'May I make a suggestion?' Doc asked. 'To give you a few minutes to think about that and also to let me ask a question or two about the suicide, which interests me, will you have a drink with me at the bar across the street?'

'Well – guess I'll have time for one. Couple little things I gotta do here first, though. If you want to go ahead I'll join you over there in ten minutes.'

At the bar, which he had investigated and found not wanting on his first day in Bartlesville, Doc ordered himself a beer and then got his pipe loaded and going. The cold beer tasted good, and he was just finishing it when the sheriff slid into the booth across from him. He said, 'Beer looks good,' and turned towards the bar and called out, 'Hey, Hank, bring us two beers. Big ones.'

And then to Doc, 'Been thinking while I crossed the street. Guess you're right about not hitting Gus with the news about the dog right now. He's pretty broke up. But – uh, did you leave the dog along the road where he might see it driving home, or where somebody else might see it and phone him?'

Doc shook his head. 'It's rolled up in a tarp in the back of my car. I'll bury it when I get home.' He relighted his pipe, which had gone out. 'Damned sorry about the dog, but I couldn't help running over it. It dashed from nowhere right under my wheels. Didn't even have time to touch the brakes before I hit it.'

'Funny,' the sheriff said. 'Buck was always afraid of cars, ran into the fields when he heard one coming. Car-shy, like some dogs are gun-shy.'

Doc stared at the sheriff. 'Good Lord, Sheriff. Then he must have been crazy, running blind and deaf. Have there been any cases of rabies around here?'

'Not in a couple of years. Longer'n that, I guess.' He seemed uninterested.

Doc stared at the big moon face, wondering whether or not the sheriff was stupid. Probably not, he decided; probably of average intelligence, but unimaginative. He could dismiss the strangeness of the actions of the field mouse and those of the dog as irrelevant and think only about the actions of the boy Tommy. They'd been peculiar, yes, but after all the boy had gone suddenly insane, and insane people do insane things. That would be the reasoning of the sheriff, and no doubt of everyone else, concerned or not concerned, who had attended the inquest.

Let's see, what had he wanted to ask the sheriff about the inquest? Yes ... 'Uh – Sheriff. I got to the inquest a little late; didn't hear the medical report. Was there an autopsy?'

'Autopsy? No, what for? Wasn't any doubt he killed himself, slashing his wrists with a knife. No other marks, except scratches on his legs, from bushes, and the bottoms of his feet cut and bloody.'

Doc opened his mouth and closed it again.

The sheriff said, 'Say, I been trying to place where you'd be staying or living out that road. House at the very end of it, about ten miles out?'

'That's right,' Doc said. 'The old Burton place, they call it; used to be a farm but it's gone wild now. Friend of mine back in Boston bought it to use as a summer vacation place.

This summer he couldn't get away and offered to let me use it.'

'Yeah, guy named – uh – Hastings. Met him a few times, summers. Wife with you, or staying alone out there?'

'I'm staying alone. Not married. I like to get a little solitude once in a while. When you teach—'

'What do you teach, Mr Staunton?'

'Call me Doc, Sheriff. I teach physics at MIT. Specialise in electronics. I've done some work on the satellite programme, too. Spent the first half of my vacation working on that, but I've got the rest of it to myself.'

'You mean you work on rockets?' There was respect in the sheriff's voice.

'Not rockets themselves. Mostly on the detectors and transmitting sets in the satellites that send back information on radiation, cosmic rays, things like that. I helped design the components for the paddlewheel satellite, for one thing. But right now I'm more interested in fishing. There's a creek about a mile east of where I live that's—'

'I know it; I've lived there. But you – and your friend that owns the house, Hastings – ought to come out here in the hunting season sometime. Plenty deer out that way, in the woods north of you.'

'Afraid I'm not much of a hunter, Sheriff. Brought along a rifle and a pistol, but just for some target practice. And a shotgun because Hastings said there might be rattlers around the place, but I haven't seen any yet. Have another beer?'

'Okay,' the sheriff said; he held up two fingers to the bartender.

'Had any other strange deaths here, Sheriff?' Doc asked.

The sheriff looked at him curiously. 'Don't know what you mean by "strange",' he said. 'Couple of unsolved killings in the last few years, but they were robbery kills, nothing strange about them.'

'No other case of anyone going suddenly suicidally – or homicidally – insane?'

'Ummm – not since I've been in office, six years almost. But what's strange about it? People *do* go crazy, don't they?'

'Yes, except that insanity usually follows certain patterns, and Tommy Hoffman's – well—'

'You're not suggesting it *wasn't* suicide, are you?'

'Of course not. Just wondering what kind of a psychosis he had, and why it hit him so suddenly, and right then. While he was, or should have been, happy and relaxed, taking a nap after – after what should have been a pretty pleasant experience. It just doesn't make sense. Well, let's skip it. You say you've fished my creek, Sheriff. What kind of fly do you use for trout?'

After he finished his second beer the sheriff said he'd better get back to Wilcox, and left. Doc ordered himself a third, and over it, and over a pipe that kept going out because he couldn't remember to keep puffing on it he lost himself in thought. Was he going overboard in thinking that the three deaths – the field mouse, the boy, the dog – formed an almost incredible sequence? The sheriff hadn't seemed to think so, but—

Or was he making much ado about nothing? A field mouse had acted strangely. First it had sat up and pawed at the boy and girl as though to warn them away. Then it had let the girl pick it up but had nipped her. When she dropped it it had started to run away and then had run back and attacked the boy, thereby in effect committing suicide.

Then the boy, Tommy Hoffman. Again, suddenly insanity starting while he was asleep or just after he awakened beside the girl, and again ending in suicide. Doc admitted that people do go insane and do commit suicide while in that state. But he'd read quite a bit about abnormal psychology and had never yet heard of a case of a person going suddenly and completely insane without having shown any preliminary symptoms and without there being some inciting cause, some traumatic experience, at the time of the onset of insanity.

Then the dog, which was where Doc had come in. Of course the dog could have had rabies, could have been running blindly and deafly – but if it hadn't, if it had been normal, then it too had in effect committed suicide by running in front of his car, especially since it had been car-shy. That was the one bit of new information he'd picked up from the sheriff, and it certainly did not make Buck's death seem more natural.

But animals, except possibly lemmings, simply do not commit suicide.

Suddenly Doc downed what little was left of his beer and knocked the dottle out of his pipe as he stood up. There were laboratories in Green Bay which could tell him whether or not Buck had been rabid; Green Bay was only forty-five miles away and it was only three o'clock in the afternoon. He had the dog's body in the station wagon and could get it there in plenty of time. Besides, he hadn't been farther from the house than the ten miles to Bartlesville in a week, and an evening in Green Bay would be a pleasant change. He could eat in a good restaurant and take in a movie if anything worth while was playing.

He did all of those things and, between leaving the dog at the laboratory – he paid in advance so he could get the report by telephone from Bartlesville late the next day – and having dinner, he picked up a dozen or so paperbacks for light reading. Strictly mystery novels. He did his serious reading at times when he was working, and read only escape literature while he was on vacation. The dinner was good; it was a change from his own cooking and better than anything he could get in Bartlesville. The movie he saw was a French farce featuring Brigitte Bardot; he had trouble following the plot but after a while gave it up and just watched Brigitte; he enjoyed the rest of it very much.

He got back a little after ten o'clock to the house at the end of the road, the house he had borrowed from his friend Hastings. It was a fair-sized house that had been a farmhouse once. There were three bedrooms upstairs, although only two of them were furnished, and a bath; there were three rooms downstairs, a big kitchen, a big living-room, and an extra room used only for storage, in which he kept his guns and fishing equipment. Electricity was provided by a generator in the basement, run by a small gasoline engine, and the same engine could be used periodically to pump water from a well to a tank on the roof. There was no telephone, but he didn't mind that; in fact, he preferred it. The area around the house and to the south of it had once been a farm, but for whatever reason it had been abandoned it had not been farmed for at least twenty years. All of it except a yard immediately around the house had gone back to brush and woods, distinguishable from the wild country north of the road only in that trees were fewer and not so tall.

It had seemed a friendly, comfortable place, until tonight.

Doc got himself a can of beer from the refrigerator and sat down to read one of the books he'd brought back, but he couldn't get interested in it. For some reason he felt uneasy. For the first time since he'd been here, he felt his isolation. He fought an impulse to pull down the shades so he couldn't be seen by anything or anybody watching from outside.

But why would *anybody* have any reason for coming way out here to the last house to look through his windows? And what did he mean by *anything*? *Anything* capable of looking through a window could only be an animal, and why should he care how many animals might be watching him? He charged himself with being ridiculous, found himself guilty as charged, and sentenced himself to opening another can of beer and trying harder to concentrate on the mystery novel.

Going back to it, he discovered that it was open at page twenty, but he couldn't remember a single thing about the previous pages he had presumably read. He started over again. It was, or should have been, an exciting mystery; there was a murder on the very first page. But he just couldn't get interested in it; between the book and his mind there interposed the story of Tommy Hoffman . . . Getting up naked, except for blue socks, from lying beside his sweetheart, and running off to a sand-floored cave; crouching in it until he saw the lanterns approaching carried by his father and his sweetheart's father, and hearing the barking of Buck, the hound. Running away from them again, circling back to a point near where he had started, picking up a rusty, broken-bladed knife and slashing his wrists, both of them.

The book was open to page fifteen now, but again he had no recollection of anything beyond the first page. He tossed it down in despair and let himself think.

He decided to try his best to put the Hoffman case out of his mind until late tomorrow afternoon when, from Bartlesville, he could phone the laboratory for the report on Buck. Then, if the dog had had rabies, which would explain *one* of the three deaths, he would put the whole thing out of his mind permanently – and enjoy the five weeks remaining of his vacation without letting himself try to solve something that was probably a coincidence instead of a mystery . . . But if Buck had *not* had rabies . . .

He had one more can of beer to make himself sleepy, and went to bed. After a while he slept.

CHAPTER SEVEN

The mind thing was still in the hollow log. He had not had himself moved since the dog had put him there the day before, and then had killed itself by running in front of the car.

Since then he had taken only one host, and that for purposes of reconnaisance. He had wanted a better picture of the surrounding country, a better one than he had gained from Tommy's mind. A bird's-eye view. So just before dawn on his first morning in his second hiding place he had entered a crow (he knew it as such from the picture of 'crow' that Tommy had had) while it was sleeping in a tree directly over him. He had tried the crow's night vision but it had been poor, so he had waited until light and then had flown it far and wide, watching through its eyes. First to the road and along it, flying high, memorising the exact location of every farmhouse he passed and, by correlating Tommy's memories, knowing the number of occupants of most of them and roughly what kind of people they were. He flew east until the road ended. Tommy had thought that the last house there was vacant, but he had been wrong; there was a station wagon parked in the cleared space in front of it.

Then the crow had circled and gone back, following the road in the other direction, all the way to Bartlesville, passing the Garner and Hoffman farms on the way. He let the crow rest a while in a tree near the edge of town, and then flew him in circles over Bartlesville, again correlating Tommy's memories with what he was seeing.

A radio and television repair shop interested him most. Surely the man who ran it would know at least something of elementary electronics and would therefore be a good host, at least for a while. But Tommy hadn't known the man's name nor where he lived, although he had known that he didn't sleep at the shop. A lot of scouting would be required to learn that; and besides, with anything less than a human host to carry him, it would be highly dangerous for him to be carried into town and hidden somewhere where the repairman would sleep within his perception range.

When he had finished with the crow he had it dive and crash into pavement; there was no use in flying it back to the woods. And his mind was immediately back in himself, in the hollow tree.

And there his mind had stayed, but it had not been idle. He had, he found, been quite fortunate in one way in his choice of this second hiding place. It was deeper in the woods and in wilder country than the cave had been. Many more creatures passed within his ken, close enough for him to study them closely. Deer had passed, and a bear. A wildcat and a skunk. Many birds, including the two he knew of, which were large enough to carry him – an owl and a chicken hawk. Air transport by day or by night, when needed. From now on anyone of those creatures could be his host any time he wanted one, as long as there was one of the variety he chose asleep within ten miles or so.

There had been smaller creatures, too, and he had studied them as well, when there was no larger one available at the same time for study. Snakes too, though they interested him little. They travelled slowly – and they died slowly. A hard-to-kill host was awkward. To be sure of killing one, he'd have to waste time crawling it to the road and waiting for a car. And even after that, even with a broken back, a snake could live quite a while.

So had passed the time until this afternoon, when something had happened, or had started to happen, that showed him he would soon have to make his next move.

He was getting hungry. More exactly, since he did not eat in the sense in which we think of eating, he was beginning to feel the need for nourishment. Time must have passed so rapidly for him back home before and during the furore that had led to his exile that he had not realised how long it had been, before his being sent here, since he had taken nourishment. This was something that he had to do only once every few months, and he had assumed that he had plenty of time to get himself established on Earth (once he had learned that there were intelligent creatures here), before he need worry about hunger; he had been wrong.

His species had evolved in water and had lived by absorbing micro-organisms from the water directly into themselves; a digestive system had never been developed. When evolution had given them shells for protection the shells had been, despite their increasing strength, sufficiently porous to let them continue to absorb nourishment as before. Before developing shells their only protection against their natural enemies had been speed. On a light-gravity planet and in the buoyant medium of water their ability to levitate, to move in any direction, had been amazingly effective as a means of escape. That, and the sense of perception, had been theirs for as far back as they had been able to trace their own evolution.

The ability to control other minds, to make other creatures their hosts, had developed later, as their intelligence had grown. It had led the more intelligent among them to quit the deeps and live close to the shore, for evolution had proceeded in a different direction on land, and there were land creatures, who sometimes slept near enough a shore to be captured as hosts, who were much more suitable as such than anything the water had produced. They had *hands* – in fact, they were not too dissimilar to our apes and monkeys – and they could, with intelligent direction, be made to do things and make things. As a man could direct an ape, if it could control the ape's mind, to do things and make things almost as efficiently as a man himself could.

With the use of suitable hosts, the mind thing's species had developed a civilisation and a science. At first they themselves had had to stay in water most of the time and operate their hosts on land. Finally they had developed a technique that eliminated that difficulty. They discovered that an occasional immersion in a nutrient solution permitted them to absorb their needed nourishment a thousand times faster and more effectively than continuous immersion in water. Now, with the help of suitable hosts, they could live as far from water as they wished and satisfy their food needs by having their hosts immerse them for an hour or so in a nutrient solution once every several months. Some of them still lived in the sea but these were relatively primitive groups, as far removed in development from their more progressive contemporaries on land as an Australian aborigine or an African Pygmy is from an atomic scientist.

But the highly civilised groups of his species had been fed by occasional immersion in a solution for so many thousands of years that they had lost the ability to live solely on what nourishment they could absorb from water. Their situation was roughly analogous to that of a human being kept alive by intravenous feeding for so many years that his digestive organs have atrophied and he can no longer survive by taking food in the manner that was once normal to him.

The mind thing could have had himself fed in the woods, using animal hosts; it is what he would have had to do if he had found no intelligent species available. But doing so, he knew, would be a long and difficult operation, involving the use of a considerable succession of hosts, each best adapted – or least poorly adapted – for one particular part of the task.

A human host working in a normally stocked kitchen could prepare an adequate nutrient solution quickly. Its exact ingredients didn't matter as long as it was rich in protein; his body would absorb only the things it needed and taste was no factor since he had no equivalent of a sense of taste. Soup stock, meat soup, or gravy would serve admirably. Even milk would serve in a pinch, although he would have to be immersed in it much longer than in a meat-rich solution.

Once he realised that he would have to take nourishment soon in any case, he decided that doing so at once and getting it over with for several months would be worth the slight risk of taking a human host sooner than he had planned to do.

He considered the choice of a human host for his purpose. Best would be someone living alone, someone who would not have to justify or explain his actions to anyone else if caught doing mysterious things in his kitchen in the middle of the night. But the nearest person he knew of living alone was Gus Hoffman, Tommy's father, and his farm was at least twice as far as the nearest one. Every extra mile he had to have himself transported increased his risk. The nearest farmhouse was occupied by only two people, an elderly couple named Siegfried and Elsa Gross. Siegfried was the dominant member of the partnership as most German husbands are; if his wife awoke and came downstairs to see what he was doing, she'd go back to the bedroom if he ordered her to.

Of course it would be better if she stayed asleep. If, while using Gross, he was forced to draw attention to him it would diminish his further usefulness – but there was always a simple answer to that.

Since the foray would be at night, an owl would be his best

means of transport. He'd test one first, of course, to make sure that it could carry his weight safely. His second choice, if the owl failed him, would be a chicken hawk, but in that case he would have to test its night vision as well as its carrying ability; it would be bad for it to fly into a tree, carrying him. If that failed – but there was no point in planning now for *all* eventualities; he would need to make alternate plans only if he found that both birds were inadequate for his purpose.

Just before dark, while most nocturnal creatures would still be sleeping, he concentrated on an owl and found himself in control of one. He was sure of getting one then, although it probably would not have been necessary. He knew enough about terrestrial creatures by now to know that, whether nocturnal or diurnal, their sleeping habits were not completely rigid. Diurnal man did most of his sleeping at night, but occasionally took naps by day – as Tommy and the girl had done. Lesser animals, since they slept more readily and more lightly, were even more prone to sleep or doze at times other than their regular sleeping periods. The dog Buck had gone to sleep in the cave, less than a minute after he had lain down there. And one of the deer that had passed near the mind thing, after browsing a while, had slept lightly on its feet for a few minutes before a sudden sound (a woodpecker in a nearby tree) had wakened it and it had moved on. No doubt the same thing was true of nocturnal creatures; after making a kill (they all seemed to be predators) and eating, they too no doubt slept or dozed a while before carrying on. He had no serious doubt that he would be able to find any kind of diurnal host sleeping somewhere by day or any nocturnal one by night, although not quite as readily as during their normal sleeping periods.

Once in control of the owl, he let it go back to sleep; he wanted it to be fully rested for the task ahead. Not until dark, when it would have done so anyway, did he let it awaken. Then he made it fly, testing the beat and strength of its wings and learning how sharply it could turn and climb. This had not mattered with the crow he had used for reconnaisance; he had simply flown it high and straight. But since the owl would be carrying him, he wanted to keep it close to the ground, flying it around trees or under their branches instead of over them. Taking the gravity of this planet into consideration – he estimated it to be about four times that of his own – he calculated that a fall of six feet would not injure him. One of twice that distance would probably be safe if he landed in grass or on soft ground. Being dropped from tree-top level would certainly be fatal unless he should be lucky enough to have a thick bush cushion his fall.

When he had satisfied himself as to the owl's manoeuvreability, which turned out to be excellent, he used its eyes to watch for a stone of suitable size, and found one. It would weigh at least as much as he, probably half again as much, and it was flattish, roughly his own shape. He had the owl alight on the stone and grip it with its talons. Take-off was difficult, but once in the air the owl flew easily with its burden, and its grip was secure. He flew it a while to make certain of that, and then let the owl drop the stone and fly to a tree near the hollow log.

He let it rest there until he judged that it was about ten o'clock – his time sense was excellent, as was his sense of direction. He estimated that the journey, since it would have to be a roundabout and zigzag course to avoid flying high, would take about an hour, and surely by eleven o'clock an elderly farm couple would be asleep.

When he thought it was time he flew the owl down and had it take him out of the hollow log. That was difficult, and for a while he thought he might have to destroy the owl so he could get another host for that purpose – perhaps a rabbit to crawl through the log from the far end and push him out; and then take another owl host for the trip. But finally he managed to have the owl reach one of its short legs far enough into the log to get a claw grip on the very end of his shell and pull him out.

The trip took longer than he had anticipated; the owl, although it flew easily with him, turned out to be less capable of sustained flight than he had realised, especially carrying a burden, and whenever he felt its wing muscles tiring he let it put him down and rest a while. Not out of consideration for the owl – he was not deliberately cruel, but simply had no empathy at all except for others of his own kind – but out of consideration for his own safety and because it would waste even more time to have to kill his host part way there and take another. He reached the Gross farm just before midnight.

He had the owl put him down in grass between the road and the farmyard fence and then fly several times around the farmhouse to reconnoitre and to choose a hiding place for himself. The house was dark and still. There seemed to be no dog on the premises, which eliminated one possible problem. And the best hiding place seemed to be under the wooden steps that led to the back door. It would have the additional advantage of being quite near the barn – before he tied himself up again by taking a human host, he would have a chance to study whatever animals might be in the barn. Thus far, except for dogs, all of his potential animal or bird hosts were wild ones; it might help on some future occasion – who knows what situation might arise? – to be able to use a domesticated animal as a host for some special purpose. As he had used the dog. There was nothing to lose except a little time that he could well afford.

He had the owl come back for him, carry him over the fence, and put him down beside the back steps. Then it pushed him under them and as far back as it could, which was far enough to put him completely out of sight.

That ended the usefulness of the owl, and he had it circle

high and then put it into a power dive to have it kill itself against the side of the house, which would be harder than the ground. He knew the thud would probably awaken the occupants, but that wouldn't matter; they'd go back to sleep sooner or later, and meanwhile he'd be able to use his sense of perception on the barn and whatever animals were inside it.

At the last second of the owl's dive, something went slightly wrong. Finding itself flying at a solid wall, the owl closed its eyes. It was an involuntary, muscular reaction, not a conscious one, and the mind thing didn't have time to correct it; he could have if he'd concentrated on keeping the eyes open. He should have anticipated it, for the same thing had happened when he had crash-dived the crow into a Bartlesville street. But that he had hardly noticed because it didn't matter. Now with the owl it mattered to the extent that, flying blind for the last second, it crashed through the pane of an upstairs window instead of hitting the outer wall of the house.

It lay inside the house, still alive but slightly stunned and with a broken wing. A light switch flicked in the next room and the door opened, letting light into the room that almost blinded the owl – but not quite; it could still see. Siegfried and Elsa Gross stood in the doorway staring, both wearing cotton flannel nightgowns.

'A damn owl,' Gross said. 'Flew right through the window. I'll get my gun and—'

'Siegried, why kill it? I mean, they kill mice and—'

The owl gathered itself, managed to get to its feet ready to attack if it had to attack to get itself killed.

The woman had taken a step towards it, but Gross said, 'Back to bed, Elsa.' Quite firmly. And then, 'It'll claw or bite you if you try to pick it up. Them things can be vicious. Besides, look, it's got a busted wing.'

They both stepped back out of sight and a moment later

the man was in the doorway again, this time with a twenty-two-calibre rifle in his hands. He aimed right between the owl's eyes.

The owl stood still for the shot.

And the mind thing was back in his shell, but still watching what was happening – this time through his perceptive sense, which was a thousand times more efficient, within its range, than sight.

Gross pushed the dead owl with the barrel of the rifle and then picked it up and dropped it outside through the broken window. He went back into their bedroom and put the rifle in a corner. His wife was already back in bed and he turned out the light and got in beside her.

'Goddamn owl,' he said, 'must have been crazy or something. Or else blind.'

'But its eyes—'

'People or animals can go blind and have their eyes look okay. 'Member the horse we had to shoot five years ago because he went blind. His eyes looked okay. Why not an owl's?' 'I guess so. Did you leave it there?'

'Threw it out the window,' Gross said. 'I'll bury it in the morning. Damn,' he grumbled again. 'Have to go in town for a pane of glass too.'

'No hurry in this weather, Siegfried,' his wife said. 'It can wait till we go in to shop next Saturday. I can tack some cheesecloth over it to keep out flies. If you had put a screen on it—'

'Why should I when we don't use the room and the window can stay shut? Besides, the owl would've gone through the screen too and I'd've had that to fix besides. Happen to notice the time while we were up?'

'Yah. A few minutes after midnight.'

'Okay, go to sleep.'

There was only silence in the bedroom and the mind thing withdrew the focus of his attention. Even if the man went to sleep right away, he wanted the woman to be sound asleep too so that, he hoped, the man could go downstairs without wakening her. He concentrated his attention in the direction of the barn.

There was a pig pen along one side of the barn and a chicken house and runway on the other, but he ignored both. A pig, he knew, was unlikely to be of any value as a host and, besides, if he ever entered one it was almost certain to be penned and so completely useless to him. The same thing was true of chickens, and either type of creature, penned in, would have considerable difficulty committing suicide or getting itself killed. It was always annoying and sometimes dangerous to be in a host that was difficult to get rid of, once it had served its purpose.

In the barn itself, besides a few mice, there were three cows, a horse, and a cat. He didn't bother studying the mice; there was nothing an ordinary mouse could do that a field mouse couldn't, and there were field mice everywhere, on farms as well as in the woods.

The cows were a little better and he took time to study one. At least they had considerable physical strength. Intelligently directed, one should be able to get out of any barn, if not by using a horn to lift a door catch, then by butting a door down; if the door was too strong for that, it could kill itself in the process of trying, so there was nothing to lose. Also, if the occasion should arise, it would be a very efficient killing machine; intelligently guided, it would be more dangerous than a bull. And one would be even easier to use by day; it dozed often while grazing or slept soundly in the shadow of a tree. And few if any fences of the kind used on farms would withstand a determined charge by a cow.

He studied the horse. It, too, could be useful in certain ways. Possibly more so than a cow. It could run faster than a cow, much faster, and it could jump a low fence or use its forefeet to batter down a higher one. And its hoofs could be as lethal as a cow's horns.

Last, the cat. As he studied it and (as he had with other animals) correlated his study with the knowledge of its characteristics and capabilities that he had learned in Tommy's mind, he gradually realised that here, for one special and important purpose, was an almost perfect host.

It could spy for him. It could go almost anywhere and hardly be noticed. It was fast and it could move silently. Its night vision was almost as good as that of an owl and, unlike an owl, it could see even better by day. Its hearing was excellent. And since there were dozens of cats between here and town and dozens more in the town itself, and since cats slept almost as much by day as by night, one would be an easy host for him to enter at any time.

He decided that, since there was plenty of time, he would try one now to determine the real extent of its capabilities. He entered the mind of the cat sleeping in the barn.

He opened its eyes. Yes, though its night vision was less than an owl's, it could see fairly well even in the almost complete darkness of the barn, relieved only by faint moonlight coming in through one open window. He guided the cat to the window, jumped it up to the window ledge and then down outside. In the moonlight, faint though it was from the thin crescent of a new moon, it could see quite well.

He ran it several times around the house, noting the silence with which it could run – scarcely a sound even on the gravel of the driveway – and checking its speed. He found that it could run very fast for short distances; for a spurt it could outdistance a dog easily, although in a sustained chase a dog would probably catch it unless it found cover or climbed a tree.

There was a tree behind the barn and he tested its climbing ability and found it excellent.

From near the top of the tree, through a space between

branches, he could see that there was a light in an upstairs window of the next farmhouse towards town. He hadn't intended to keep the cat that long or take it that far, but here was an excellent chance to test its capabilities as a spying tool.

He brought the cat down from the tree and trotted it across the fields to the other farmhouse. The cat moved like a shadow in the night.

When he reached the farmhouse he saw that there were two windows lighted, both obviously windows of the same room, an upstairs corner room at the front of the house. The window he had seen from the tree on the Gross farm was the side one; the other was just above a front porch roof. There was a tree near the porch and the cat climbed it and jumped lightly from a branch to the porch roof, up its slight slope to the window and then to the outside window sill.

Its eyes adjusted quickly to looking into the lighted room. A child was lying in bed, coughing hoarsely. A woman in a bathrobe and slippers was bending over the child and a gaunt man in rumpled pyjamas stood in the doorway. From their conversation – audible to the cat even though the window was closed – the mind thing learned that the child had croup; the man was asking the woman whether she thought she could take care of it or whether he should phone for Doctor Gruen.

The scene itself was of no interest to the mind thing, but he now knew that he had been right in assessing the value of the cat as a host perfect for spying, for fact-finding.

Had it not been for his need to nourish himself he would have kept the cat as a host overnight and used it the next day to widen his knowledge of the other farmhouses, even sent it into the town, perhaps to follow the proprietor of the television repair shop home from work to find out where he slept. But feeding himself came first, and there was no dearth of other cats he could use later at leisure.

His problem now was to get rid of this one. He'd been in it an hour now, longer than he'd intended. He examined the cat's thoughts to find the quickest and surest way of getting it killed, and found a ready answer.

On this farm there was a vicious dog that was kept chained in a corner of the barn. (Why, he wondered, would anyone keep a dog that had to be kept chained, which made it valueless as a watchdog? But that didn't matter now.)

He took the cat down from the porch roof by way of the tree, and ran it around the back to the barn. Again there was an open window. The dog started barking fiercely the moment the cat jumped up to the sill of the window. The cat waited a moment until its eyes became accustomed to the greater darkness inside the barn, until it could see the dog clearly. Then it jumped down inside, ran to the dog, and jumped lightly into the dog's jaws.

CHAPTER EIGHT

The mind of the mind thing, back in his own body under the back steps of the Gross farmhouse, probed the house, this time carefully to make sure that there was no other living creature in the house besides Gross and his wife – such as a dog that might bark and wake the woman when Gross came downstairs. There was no dog; only a canary bird in a covered cage in the downstairs room that would be their living-room or parlour. His host would not have to go into that room.

In their upstairs bedroom Siegfried and Elsa Gross were both sleeping deeply.

The mind thing entered Gross's mind and again there was that terrible but brief struggle that always happened when he took over an intelligent entity. Disappointingly, it was briefer than had been the struggle in the mind of the boy Tommy. Was his new host even less intelligent than the boy who had failed a year of high school and who knew nothing and cared less about science, unless farming could be called a science? He'd hoped for more, from an older man, but it seemed that he'd been wrong. Gross, he saw at once, knew and cared even less about such things than Tommy Hoffman had. His education had stopped at the sixth grade and he knew little of anything outside his own farm. He didn't even own a radio and his only reading was a weekly paper and one magazine on farming, both of which he read with some difficulty.

The mind thing didn't move his host right away; he had Gross lie still until he had oriented himself in Gross's mind and had learned a few things he wanted to know before moving.

He got the answers immediately to two important questions, and both were satisfactory. First, Elsa Gross was a sound sleeper; no noise less than the owl had made crashing through the window in the next room would be likely to waken her. In the kitchen, which was not under this room, he need use only normal precautions against making noise, and not drop anything. Second, there was a quart jar of soup stock in the refrigerator, also half a bowl of rich beef gravy. Mixed together and warmed slightly – which would dissolve the probably partly solidified gravy and also enable him to absorb nourishment more readily – they would make a perfect nutrient solution. If they had not been there, and if there were no reasonable equivalent in canned goods, he would have had to use meat of some kind and cook it an hour or two to obtain a broth that still would not have been as rich as the stock and gravy combination.

That was all he needed to know for now, he decided; the rest – whatever else of interest to him might be in Gross's knowledge – he could examine at leisure later. He'd still be in the old man's mind while his body absorbed nourishment for an hour or so from the nutrient solution.

Under the mind thing's direction, Siegfried Gross slid quietly out of bed and tiptoed barefoot to the door of the room. He opened it and closed it from the outside as quietly as he could, felt his way through darkness to the stairs, and went down them. He didn't turn on a light until he was in the kitchen.

Working as quietly as possible, he got the jar and the bowl from the refrigerator. He poured the soup stock from the jar into a pan, one large enough to hold the shell of the mind thing, scraped the gravy into it from the bowl, and stirred the two together. He used a match to light a burner of the butane gas stove and put the pan over a low flame. He stirred the mixture as it warmed, occasionally testing the temperature by taking a sip from the spoon.

When the gravy was all dissolved and the temperature was right – quite warm, for the mind thing, protected by his shell, could stand quite a range of temperature, from fifty or more degrees below zero almost to the boiling point of water – he turned off the flame under the pan.

He went outside, leaving the kitchen door open to give himself light, reached back under the steps and found the mind thing. He carried it inside and placed it carefully in the liquid in the pan.

Then, after taking a look at the kitchen clock so he could time the operation, Siegfried Gross sat down to wait. While he waited, in Gross's mind the mind thing sorted out his knowledge and his memories.

What he learned was far from encouraging when he considered keeping his present host for any purpose other than his current one.

Siegfried Gross, at sixty-five, was a bitter and lonely man. He was on civil terms with some of his neighbours and with some of the merchants in the town, but he had no friends. He loved no one and no one loved him, not even his wife; there had been no affection between them for many years. They had stayed together for the simple reason that they needed one another, for different reasons. Elsa had no relatives to whom she could go, no way of earning a living on her own; Siegfried needed her help to run the house and to do certain chores allotted to her around the barn. And they tolerated one another; there was no hatred.

They had two children, one son and one daughter, but Siegried had quarrelled with both of them when, during their respective late teens, they had decided to leave the farm and go to the city. Each had written a few letters to

Elsa, but Siegfried had forbidden her to answer them, and they no longer even knew where their children lived.

His future looked black because for several years he had been slowly developing arthritis, and it was progressive. He had no faith in doctors, and they probably would not have been able to help him much anyway. Already it was painful for him to do his work, and he knew that after a few more years of increasing pain he would have to give up working and sell the small farm. He owned it clear and would perhaps get enough for it to buy his and Elsa's way into a home of some sort for the rest of their lives, but that was all he had to look forward to – that, and the slowly increasing pain which would eventually cripple him completely, if he lived that long.

Part of the bitterness that had been with him all his life lay in the fact that he hated his country and its government. It was, in fact, only technically his country; he thought of himself as a German rather than as an American. His parents had brought him from Germany when he was only four years old. They had become naturalised citizens, for practical reasons only, which had made him a citizen too. But their true loyalty remained towards the old country, and so did his. He had spoken no English until he started to school at seven. He had been in his early twenties when the United States had entered World War I. They had tried to draft him and he had spent a miserable year and a half interned as a conscientious objector; actually he had no objection, conscientious or otherwise, to war. He had given that as his reason; but he had simply not wanted to fight on what to him was the wrong side.

He had welcomed the renascence of Germany under Hitler and had become an ardent Nazi, although he had never joined a Bund or any other group. When the United States got into the second war his opinions and his expression of them became even more violent. By then he was in his middle forties and there was no question of his being drafted, but he was also by then more intransigent and less discreet than he had been in his younger days. There was talk of putting him in a concentration camp, but the authorities decided that, however verbally violent, he was harmless and was in no position to sabotage the war effort. Besides, if all Nazi sympathisers in Wisconsin had been put into a concentration camp, it would have required one the size of a Wisconsin county to hold them.

Often, during the war and after it, he thought bitterly of his son, who had left home shortly before the war had started. His son and his daughter had considered themselves Americans; that had been one thing, besides their wanting to leave the farm, that his quarrels with them had been about. Had his son let himself be drafted – or even volunteered – to fight against the Fatherland? If so, he hoped that he had been killed.

During the war, to follow the news, he had subscribed to a daily newspaper and had bought a radio. After Hitler's defeat he cancelled the former, and vented his anger on the latter with an axe.

Always he had wanted someday, even if he had to wait until he retired, to return to the Fatherland. But always, at times when it might have been possible financially for him to do so, there had been reasons why he could not. Now he knew that it was no longer possible. He was fated to die in this foreign land in which he had already lived over sixty years, among strangers. Completely among strangers since the first years of his married life and since his parents' deaths.

In one way, and only one, had he compromised with this alien land: he spoke English and had almost lost his German. At first he and Elsa had spoken German, but she, so obedient in every other way, had been adamant, after their children were born, that only English be spoken. If he spoke to her in their own tongue, she answered him in the foreign one. Since he was no teacher, the children had never learned more than a few phrases of German, and he himself had gradually acquiesced and come to use the language he knew almost as well as the one he considered his own.

These facts about his host the mind thing bothered to learn only because he had time to kill while his own body absorbed nourishment, and because anything, however trivial, that concerned the mores and thought processes of human beings that he could learn might some day serve him. He had no sympathy for a host's despair or his problems; he was concerned only with a host's usefulness. And he had already decided that Siegfried Gross would be useless to him after tonight.

Gross was a recluse; he had no real communication with anyone else, no way of gathering information that would not be completely out of character for him and which would not arouse comment and curiosity. He had no telephone, wrote no letters, and received no personal mail. He rode into Bartlesville – in a wagon behind a horse; he'd never owned or wanted an automobile – once a week on Saturday afternoon to do whatever buying was necessary. Never oftener than that except during certain seasons when he had produce to take in to sell, something that could not wait until his next Saturday trip. He went only to certain places, and even in them he never stopped to talk or to listen to gossip or news. He had not been farther from his farm than the five miles into Bartlesville in over fifteen years – since, in fact, Germany had gone down in defeat for the second time in his lifetime.

No, Siegfried Gross, kept in character and made to act naturally, would be the worst information-finding instrument he could possibly have chosen. He was serving his purpose now, and when that purpose was finished, he must go.

Besides, the mind thing had already discovered tonight his perfect host for the gathering of information – the cat. As long as he kept Gross, he could not use cats, but one of them would eventually lead him to the human being nearby, in or out of Bartlesville, best adapted to be his host, for whatever period of usefulness. There was no hurry, now that he was being fed.

But while Gross sat waiting, the mind thing knew that he might as well gain from Gross's mind what little it did know about his neighbours. He did learn a few facts, although none of them seemed of immediate importance. Gross knew much less about his neighbours in general than Tommy Hoffman had known. And he had not yet learned of Tommy's suicide and the inquest; he probably would not have learned of it until his next Saturday trip into town.

The mind thing did learn, though, the answer to a question that had mildly puzzled him earlier: why Gross's nearest neighbour would keep a dog so vicious that it had to be kept chained in the barn. His neighbours were the Loursats (a French name, but they were of Belgian extraction). The dog was a Labrador retriever bitch, a fairly valuable dog that John Loursat used for duck hunting. Before it had suddenly turned vicious – towards everyone but Loursat himself – he had it bred to another good Labrador and was due to have a litter within a few weeks. Since it had attacked Loursat's wife – fortunately it had not bitten her – it was under sentence of death, but Loursat was hoping that it would not turn on its puppies when it had them and that he could let it nurse them long enough to salvage the litter before he had to shoot the dog. He had chained it in an unused corner of the barn and had given strict orders that neither his wife nor daughter was to go near it. Gross had happened to know this because Loursat, one of the neighbours with whom he was still on civil terms, had asked him if he wanted one of the puppies and, even when Gross had refused, went on to explain about them and why he would want to find homes for them as quickly as he could. Gross did not like dogs any more than he liked people; he tolerated a cat, so long as it lived in the barn, because it killed mice there.

Through Gross's eyes the mind thing looked at the clock and decided that he had been in the solution long enough; he had to decide it on a basis of timing because while in a host's mind he had no sensation in his own body.

Gross stood up and took the shell out of the now cooled solution and started with it towards the outer door. Then the thing in his mind had an afterthought and he turned back to the sink. He rinsed the shell off very thoroughly and dried it. The mind thing's afterthought had been that the odour of the solution might attract some animal and cause it to crawl under the steps and draw attention to them, perhaps even drag the mind thing out from under them. He himself had no odour whatsoever. He knew that from having been in the mind of the dog Buck when the dog had dug him up in the cave and moved him to the hollow log.

Gross carried him outside, again leaving the door wide to give himself a little light. The mind thing made his hiding place even safer by having Gross scoop out some dirt under the steps and bury him an inch or so deep, smoothing the ground carefully. Then from the steps he reached down and smoothed out the marks of his bare feet on the ground beside the steps.

Then he went inside to die.

But first he cleaned up the evidence of what he had been doing; he poured the rest of the solution down the drain and washed the three things he had used. He put the pan and the gravy bowl back where they belonged, the empty glass jar with other empty jars. Of course Elsa might miss the stock and the gravy and wonder a little, but there was nothing he could do about that. Besides, she was getting absent-minded lately and knew it; she'd probably think she'd used the stock and the gravy and forgotten about it. Then, too, there'd be the shock of his death to distract her from trivia. Although she wouldn't grieve for him, any sudden event that changes one's life is a shock. Later she'd come to realize that she was better off for his having killed himself. What the sale of the farm would bring would be much better provision for the old age of one person than of two.

Should he mention that in his suicide note? For a suicide note there was going to be, this time. That lesson the mind thing had learned from Tommy's death; it had aroused too much curiosity, enough to send Hoffman and Garner to the cave, even to make them decide to dig there. He wanted Gross's suicide to appear to be perfectly normal, fully motivated, so it would arouse no curiosity at all.

He had Gross get a writing tablet and a pencil and sit down at the kitchen table with them. Then he gave thought to how Gross would word a suicide note if he genuinely decided to kill himself. He would not have and would not mention any such unselfish motive as leaving more money for Elsa's old age. And his note, if he wrote one at all, would be short and to the point, with no apologies and no goodbyes.

Gross wrote slowly and laboriously, in a handwriting that still looked more like German script than English, although the words were English, spelled as Gross would have spelled them.

'I cant stand pane from artherites anny more. I kill myself.'

He signed his name in full and then, under it, a final defiance, in German, to the country he hated. His last word. 'Deutschland über Alles.'

Then he got his shotgun from the kitchen closet, loaded it, and sat down at the table again. He put the muzzle in his mouth, pointing upwards, and pulled the trigger. Blood and brain matter splattered the note on the top page of the writing tablet, but the words were still legible.

Back in his own body, well hidden under the steps, the

mind thing, able again to use his perceptive sense, heard Elsa cry out her husband's name upstairs. He watched her turn on the bedroom light, then the hall light, and come down the stairs.

CHAPTER NINE

Doc Staunton awoke slowly, turned over, and raised his arm to look at his wrist watch. It was after ten, which was not surprising since he'd got to bed pretty late the night before. He'd gone into Bartlesville later the previous afternoon so the time would be right for him to phone the laboratory in Green Bay about the dog. He'd phoned them and had learned what, he realised now, he'd known all along he would learn.

The dog Buck had not had rabies. Nor had he had, aside from the injuries that had caused his death, anything organically wrong with him that could be determined by dissection. The dog's having run in front of the car couldn't be explained by anything ascertainably physically wrong with him.

Doc had sighed, and had phoned into Wilcox to try to reach the sheriff. The sheriff would be interested, or at least he should be interested. But the sheriff wasn't available and his office didn't know where he was. Doc had stayed in town for dinner at the better – such as it was – of the two local restaurants. Then he'd tried to reach the sheriff again, this time first at his office and then at his home number. He got no answer at the former and no satisfaction at the latter.

He'd killed a little time in the tavern and had been enlisted in a poker game starting in the back room. One of the local merchants, Hans Weiss, the grocer from whom he bought most of his supplies, had invited him and vouched for him. There were only four others, counting Hans, ready to start the game and they'd need a fifth. The stakes were just enough to make the game interesting; nickel ante, fifty-cent limit. Doc lost twelve dollars in the first half hour without winning a hand, then a big hand put him ahead and he stayed that way. Twice, once around eight o'clock and once around nine, he tried to reach the sheriff and failed. The next time he happened to look at his watch it was almost midnight and he decided it was too late to try again that night. By that time there were seven in the game and he was the big winner, about seventy dollars ahead, so he didn't think he should quit until someone else suggested breaking up the game. That hadn't happened until one-thirty and he'd got home at two, still forty-some dollars to the good. And he'd become a friend of everyone in the game and had accepted an invitation to play again. After all, he had to give the boys a chance to win their money back. As a comparative stranger in their midst, that was the least he could do.

Now, Thursday morning, he yawned and got up. Might as well get into Bartlesville before noon and phone the sheriff; he could make an appointment, if the sheriff was free, to drive on into Wilcox to see him. Unless, of course, the sheriff was coming into Bartlesville anyway; then he could ask the sheriff to have lunch with him.

He made himself only coffee for breakfast and got into town by half-past eleven, where he phoned the sheriff from the drugstore. This time he connected.

'Doc Staunton, Sheriff,' he said. 'Something I wanted to talk to you about, if you can spare me a few minutes. You coming here anyway, or shall I drive in to Wilcox and come to your office?'

'You caught me just as I was leaving, Doc. For Bartlesville.'

'Good. Can you have lunch with me, then?'

'Guess so. Sure, thanks. Which restaurant?'

Doc said, 'Let's meet at the tavern first. One drink won't hurt us, if we're eating right afterwards.'

The sheriff agreed and said he'd be there within half an hour.

Doc walked from the wall phone to the drug counter to make a few purchases. The druggist was one of the men with whom he'd played poker last night and they greeted each other by name.

'Heard you call the guy you were talking to "Sheriff", Doc,' the druggist said. 'Nothing wrong, I hope?'

'No. Just want to pass on some information to him.'

'Not about our poker games, I hope. Say, Doc, you live out the Bascombe Road, don't you?'

Doc nodded. 'I've wondered why they call it that, but I do. Last house. Why?'

'Another suicide out your way, last night. Or maybe you heard about it already?'

Something prickled at the back of Doc's neck. 'No, I hadn't. Just got in town; this is my first stop. Who was it?'

'Old geezer by the name of Siegfried Gross. Not much loss; nobody liked him and he liked everybody even less than that. He lives – lived – about five miles out from town. That'd be about three miles from your place.'

Doc probed but found out only two things more: that Gross had killed himself with a shotgun sometime in the middle of the night, and that he had left a suicide note saying he was killing himself because of the pain of his arthritis.

He put his drugstore purchases in his car and strolled thoughtfully to the tavern. Mike, the bartender, was talking with two customers about the suicide of Gross, but none of them knew any more than Doc had already learned from the druggist.

Doc nursed a beer until the sheriff came in, then he

downed what was left of it and he and the sheriff took the booth they'd sat in after the inquest.

'No beer for me this time,' the sheriff said wearily. 'I can use a pickup, Mike. Double bourbon, water on the side.' Doc said he'd settle for another beer and Mike went back to the bar.

The sheriff yawned. 'Guess you heard about Siegfried Gross,' he said. 'I had to go out there in the middle of the night and ain't slept since. Gawd, but I'm tired. And soon as we eat I got to go out there again.'

'Mind if I go with you?' Doc asked.

'If you want. Was it something about the Gross business you wanted to tell me, Doc?'

'No, I didn't even know of it when I phoned you. It's about the Hoffman dog. It did not have rabies.'

The sheriff raised bushy eyebrows. 'You mean you had it checked? What for, it didn't bite nobody. Or did it?'

'No, it bit no one. But I was curious, especially after you told me it was car-shy, why it ran blindly in front of my car. If it had been rabid, that would have explained it.'

'Hell, Doc, dogs get run over every day. He was probably tracking a rabbit that crossed the road there, had his nose down and wasn't watching. You can't make a supreme court case out of a dog getting itself run over.'

'I suppose not, but— Sheriff, was there anything unusual in connection with Gross's suicide?'

'It was plenty messy. Put the barrel of a shotgun in his mouth and pulled the trigger, blew his brains all over the place. Took our mortician friend over an hour to clean up that kitchen. Lord, what a mess.'

'Will there be an inquest?'

'With a suicide note in his own writing, what for? Just a waste of taxpayers' money. Well, let's have one more quick one and then go and eat, huh?'

It wasn't until over dessert and coffee that Doc again

asked if there had been any unusual circumstances, anything at all, in connection with the suicide.

'Funny thing or two happened the same night, but nothing to do with the suicide,' the sheriff said. 'An owl flew through the window, through the glass, I mean, around midnight, and Gross had to shoot it because it had a busted wing.'

'With the same shotgun?'

'Hell, no. Used a twenty-two rifle for that. And it was maybe three hours after that he killed himself, but I figure he couldn't go back to sleep and laid there suffering and finally decided to put himself out of his misery like he'd done to the owl, and went down to the kitchen and did it.'

Doc frowned. 'Was there any physical contact between Gross and the owl?'

'Not till after it was dead. After he shot it Gross tossed it out through the busted window and told his wife he'd bury it in the morning.' The sheriff stopped to take a swallow of his coffee. 'Loursat, that's the guy next door, buried it. And the cat. Sometime in the night Gross's cat got in Loursat's barn and a vicious dog there killed it.'

Doc Staunton took a deep breath. He said softly, so softly that the sheriff could barely hear it, ' "The Owl and the Pussycat went to sea, in a beautiful pea-green boat." '

'Huh?'

'Line from a nonsense poem by Edward Lear. Sheriff, have you ever known an owl to fly through a pane of glass before?'

'Dunno about an owl especially, Doc, but birds fly into glass all the time. Got a picture window in my house that a bird flies into – oh, maybe one or twice a week. Mostly sparrows. Usually just stun themselves a minute, but once in a while one breaks its neck. Well, guess we're ready. You want to ride out with me, or go in separate cars so you can go on home after?'

CHAPTER TEN

The mind thing had learned much that surprised him.

Since the suicide of Siegfried Gross he had spent most of the time deliberately hostless so he could stay within himself under the steps and use his perceptive senses to see and hear all that went on inside the Gross farmhouse or near it.

He learned above all that he had been careless, and had aroused curiosity by the things he had made his hosts, human or animal, do, especially by the manner in which he had made them kill themselves.

He had had no idea of the fuss and bother caused by a human suicide, even when the suicide left a note saying that he was killing himself. What had happened in the Gross house since Siegfried's suicide in the kitchen had been a revelation to him in human mores.

It had started immediately after the shotgun blast. Elsa Gross had come running down the stairs, and had been a good deal more excited and disturbed than he had anticipated, having known from Gross's mind that there was no real love between them.

Her initial shock had been tremendous. After the worst of it had worn off she had put her shoes on and a coat over her nightgown and had run out of the house and started off in the direction of the nearest neighbours, the Loursats, through whose window he had earlier seen the man and woman in the bedroom of the sick child. It was their vicious dog that had obligingly freed him from his cat host by killing the cat.

Elsa Gross had come back about half an hour later and Loursat had been with her. From their conversation the mind thing had learned that Loursat had phoned the sheriff and that he would be there within an hour; Loursat had come back with her to await the sheriff's coming. His wife would have come too, except that she had to stay with the sick child, who was better, but still shouldn't be left alone.

Loursat suggested that Elsa Gross go upstairs and dress, and while she did this he examined the kitchen as thoroughly as he could without stepping into any of the blood splatters. He read the suicide note several times and shook his head. But he didn't touch it or anything else in the kitchen.

Then he went into the living-room – still well within range of the mind thing's perception – and waited there until Elsa Gross came down. There in the living-room, out of sight of the thing in the kitchen, they talked.

The mind thing learned that, despite the note, Elsa Gross was bewildered by her husband's sudden suicide. He had had arthritis, yes, but it just couldn't have been bad enough to make him want to kill himself because of it. Why, he'd been perfectly normal and not in pain at all around midnight when the owl had wakened them up flying through the window. Loursat had asked her about that and she'd told him what had happened.

'Funny about the owl,' Loursat said. 'Never knew one to do that before. Wonder if there's some kind of craziness going around. Like – you've heard about Tommy Hoffman, haven't you?'

She hadn't, and he told her.

It was a little after three o'clock in the morning when the sheriff came in an ambulance and brought with him the coroner and the mortician.

From all the questions and conversations, the mind thing was learning how seriously human beings took the suicide of one of themselves, even when the suicide left a note to explain his reasons.

The next day he learned even more. Neighbours dropped in to sympathise with Mrs Gross and to offer their help. Loursat came again, this time with the bad news that the Gross cat had somehow got inside his barn and that his dog, despite being chained in a corner, had killed it. Then more neighbours called and *that* became a topic of conversation.

At noon Mrs Gross had missed the gravy and the soup stock. The mind thing knew she had missed them, or at least one of them, because she searched the refrigerator thoroughly, moving everything in it behind which a bowl or jar could have been hidden.

Shortly after noon the sheriff had come back, this time bringing a different man with him. He told Mrs Gross that there would have to be an inquest, although with the suicide note it would be just a formality and wouldn't take long. He suggested having it the next afternoon, at the mortuary, and told her he'd pick her up in his car to take her there and bring her home again afterwards. While she was there she could make arrangements with the mortician for the funeral.

Then he had introduced the man who had come with him as a Mr Staunton. He said Mr Staunton was a scientist who was vacationing near Bartlesville, and that he had become interested in the completely mysterious suicide of Tommy Hoffman and had been trying to find a satisfactory explanation for it. And now, because of the coincidence of another suicide happening so soon after and so near the first one, he was curious about that too, and would like to talk to her about it if she was willing.

Mrs Gross had been willing to talk; she even insisted on making coffee for them, since she said she hadn't bothered making any just for herself to go with her lunch.

Mr Staunton was a small wiry man, somewhere in his fifties, with iron grey hair in a short crew cut and with dancing, piercing bright blue eyes.

His curiosity was almost insatiable. He must have asked at least a hundred questions, and Elsa Gross answered all of them. A question about whether anything else unusual had happened brought out the death of the cat and the missing items from the refrigerator. And then he'd asked a lot of questions about each of those matters. He seemed both excited and puzzled.

The mind thing was learning most of all how greatly he had underestimated the curiosity of human beings. Of course his only direct knowledge of their attitudes had come from an immature and incurious mind – Tommy had never been interested in problems and had simply accepted the world as he saw it – and from the rigid and dogmatic mind, phlegmatic and intractable, of a man who had cared nothing about anything outside his own narrow world and opinions.

The mind of this little man Staunton, so far as the mind thing could judge it from the questions he asked and his manner in listening to their answers, was something else again, a revelation. And he was, the sheriff had mentioned, a scientist. What kind of scientist? Probably, from the questions he'd asked, not one of the physical sciences; but even so, might he not make a better next host than the television repairman in Bartlesville, who after all would be more of a mechanic than a scientist?

Too late, just as Staunton and the sheriff were leaving, it came to him that he should keep track of this possibly desirable host, learn where he lived, and investigate his possibilities. When he thought of it they were almost outside his range of perception, on the way towards the car or cars they had left on the road, and he quickly tried to think of a host he might find near enough to be able to follow the car the man Staunton would get into.

The horse in the barn was his first thought, but he rejected it instantly, even though the horse did happen to be dozing at the moment. As has been said, he was learning much. The horse might have broken out of the barn and been able to follow the car, but for it to do so would have been completely outside the pattern of a horse's normal actions, and he knew now that whenever he drew attention to one of his hosts by having it perform an uncharacteristic act, he thereby endangered his own project. Horses simply did not go breaking out of barns and chasing automobiles to their destinations.

He thought of a bird. First of a chicken hawk, because it was fast, but none was sleeping within his range. Then of an owl, because it would be sleeping by day – but he discarded the thought quickly when he realised that an owl was much too slow a flier to keep up with an automobile.

Then he thought of a sparrow; he didn't know a sparrow's flying speed, but sparrows were plentiful and even by day he'd surely find one asleep somewhere nearby.

The sparrow he chose had been sleeping in a tree about two hundred yards back from the house. As he circled up into the air he saw that he was too late; the two cars that had been parked on the road in front of the farm were driving off in opposite directions, each already almost a quarter of a mile away. Too far, even, through a sparrow's eyes, to be able to identify either car if he should ever see it again. Besides, he could see now that a sparrow could not possibly have kept up with a car.

He was careful in getting rid of his host. He flew it across the road and deep into the woods before he flew it head-on into a tree; and he remembered the involuntary closing of the owl's eyes and concentrated on keeping the sparrow's open. Even so, the attempt to kill the bird was not immediately successful; a twig too small to be seen at the speed at which it was flying deflected it, and instead of breaking its neck it broke a wing and lay helpless under the tree.

Since there was no alternative to patience, he was patient. The sparrow would die of hunger or thirst, if one of its enemies did not find it. And he himself, his shell, was safe under the steps at the back door of the Gross farm. He perceived but did not feel his host's pain; pain was something he could feel and understand only in himself, in his own body. Such pain could come from extremes of heat or cold, but extremes far greater than occurred on this particular planet. Or it could come at the moment of death if his shell were ever broken, or even cracked.

There was no hurry about anything, now that he had taken nourishment and would not have to do so again for months. He expected confidently to have possession by then of a really suitable host who had the knowledge, the money, and the ability to build him the electronic machine that would get him home. No one of those things would be of much value, without the others – unless he used a succession of hosts, and that would be awkward, and dangerous.

He thought of reproducing himself, a voluntary process with his species, but immediately discarded it as impractical. Once the process of fission was started it could not be stopped, and for a long while he would be helplessly schizophrenic, in partial control of each of the two parts into which his shell would be forming, in insufficient control of either part to be able to take or direct a host. It was a penalty his species had paid for their highly specialised evolution, this state of helplessness during reproduction; each part needed the help of another or others of his kind to direct a host or hosts to care for him during a period of almost a terrestrial year.

On only a few planets could a member of his species propagate alone; there were a few, a very few, moderately intelligent races in the galaxy which accepted host status willingly and could be trained in advance to continue to care for a mind thing during the period when he was helpless to keep a host under control.

He was resigned to waiting out the death of the sparrow even if it took days, but shortly after full dark he heard the flutter of an owl's wings overhead. He fluttered his own good wing to attract its attention, and the owl saw and flew down. Less than a minute later its cruel beak had killed the crippled sparrow, and the mind thing was back in his shell, on the Gross farm.

He was just in time to hear knocking at the door and to see – with his perceptive sense that made things simultaneously visible and transparent – the sheriff standing outside the front door and Elsa Gross going to open it. She was taking off a white apron that she was wearing over a plain black dress. Mrs Gross would not have to spend money for mourning clothes, the mind thing knew from the contents of her closet upstairs. Almost all of her 'good' clothes were black already.

'Evening, ma'am,' the sheriff said, when she had opened the door. 'Came out to take you in to see the undertaker, if you're ready to go.'

'Thanks, Sheriff, but Mr Loursat next door was here. He's coming in half an hour to take me in. Didn't he phone you? He said he would.'

'Probably tried but didn't reach me. Been lots of places, but not home or back to the office.' He took off his hat and rubbed the top of his balding head. 'Well, if you don't need me—'

'Won't you come in anyway, just for a minute? Maybe have a cup of coffee? It's still hot, I think.'

'Well – guess I could use a cup. All right, thanks.'

She stepped back and he followed her in and closed the door.

'You set there, Sheriff.' Mrs Gross indicated a comfortable chair. 'I'll bring us each a cup. Cream and sugar?'

'Just a little sugar.'

She came back a moment later, handed the sheriff a cup, and sat down with another one in her lap. 'Is it still hot enough?'

The sheriff took a sip. 'Just fine. I don't like it *too* hot. Ma'am, have you made any plans? I mean, you don't intend to try and run the farm yourself, do you? I guess you could, with a hired hand, but—'

'I'm getting a little old for that, I guess, Sheriff. No, if I can sell the farm, I will. And maybe it's sold already, kind of.'

'Who to, if I may ask, ma'am?'

'Mr Loursat's got a brother, working in Menominee. He's a machinist but he was raised on a farm and likes farming; he's been talking about getting himself a little one instead of working in a town. Mr Loursat's going to write him about it. They're close to one another, and he thinks his brother will jump at a chance to get a farm next to his. He says, too, he can raise enough money to lend his brother for a down payment if he hasn't got that much saved.'

'Sounds like a good idea, ma'am.'

'Yes, it does. And if it takes a little while to work out, I've got enough help to get me by, at least till the end of school vacation. Mr Karmer, who owns the farm on the other side, has a boy in high school, doing nothing this summer but helping his father. He dropped in to tell me the boy's a good worker and would work half days for me if I wanted, the rest of the summer.'

'Sounds fine, ma'am. Looks like you'll make out all right. Plan to live in town? Here, I mean, in Bartlesville?'

'I – haven't decided yet.'

'Don't I remember you got a son and a daughter?'

'I had. But Siegfried quarrelled with them both, and wouldn't let me write to either. And they gave up writing, it's been over ten years now.'

'You don't know the last addresses?'

'Not street addresses. Bertha was in Cincinnati, Max was in Milwaukee. But that was ten years ago.'

The sheriff smiled. 'Knew if I kept asking questions I'd find something I could do for you. I'll write the chief of police in both places. They'll be able to find a lead to at least one of them, maybe as easy as looking in the phone book. And if you find one, you'll find both; they're probably in touch with one another.'

'Thank you, Sheriff.' Mrs Gross smiled, but then suddenly there were tears running down her cheeks.

Another knock, Loursat's, sent her to the door, hastily wiping her eyes and her cheeks as she went.

Within ten minutes they had all gone; the sheriff first and, a few minutes later, Mrs Gross and Loursat; he had waited to show her the letter he had just written to his brother in Menominee, Michigan, which he intended to mail while they were in town.

The mind thing considered.

He had plenty of time to consider, during the two hours she was away, and afterwards when she had gone to bed and to sleep.

He planned. Now that he knew *her* plans, Elsa Gross was a possible next host. He planned ahead, but tentatively, contingent upon two ifs. One, that she should be able, as she hoped, to sell the farm. Two, that by that time – which would no doubt be a few weeks hence – the sheriff would have been able to locate either her daughter or her son, in Cincinnati or in Milwaukee – or for that matter, elsewhere, if elsewhere turned out to be any relatively major city.

She was asleep now and he could have taken over, but he didn't; he could wait – she'd be sleeping here every night for at least a couple of weeks. And after all, there was the possibility things wouldn't work out as she had planned; maybe Loursat's brother wouldn't want the farm, and maybe the sheriff would be unable to locate either her son or her daughter. Also, it would be bad to have to make her kill herself here, even if he could arrange to make it look like an accident; two deaths by violence would draw altogether too much interest to the farm.

But he could wait, and plan while he waited, always taking a better chance in another direction if he could find one. The sheriff would be an excellent next host, better than Elsa Gross even if her plans worked out; the sheriff could find reason any time to take a trip to Milwaukee and would have complete freedom of movement there to investigate things and people the mind thing would want investigated. And the sheriff drove a car, so it would be easy to get him killed when he had served his purpose; he could simply have a head-on collision in such a way that it would be presumed that he had gone to sleep at the wheel, or blacked out. If the sheriff turned out to be a drinking man, so that getting drunk wouldn't be too out of character for him, it could be worked that way.

But getting the sheriff for a host was an outside chance, in any case. He lived, and slept, in the county seat. In Wilcox, not in Bartlesville. That was too far for the mind thing to risk having himself transported there by an animal host.

Meanwhile, though, he could expand his knowledge of the countryside and the nearby town, and of the inhabitants of the town. The radio-television repairman had turned out to be a poor prospect, but there might be better ones. Even if not, one could not have too much knowledge.

So – the cats. The silent-footed, keen-eared cats that made such perfect spy-hosts.

The mind thing concentrated upon the concept *cat.*

CHAPTER ELEVEN

Friday morning was cloudy in Bartlesville, and just before noon a slight drizzle of rain started to fall. Willie Chandler looked out of the window of his radio and television repair shop and was glad he'd brought a lunch and wouldn't have to walk to the restaurant.

It was about the only thing he was glad about.

Business was poor and he was head over heels in debt. He'd made a bad mistake, three years ago, in believing that Bartlesville was large enough to support a repair shop for radio and television sets. Every family, almost, had a radio – but it was very seldom that anything went wrong with one. And there were few television sets; it was possible to get reception from Green Bay, but it was not too satisfactory at that distance. Even the few people who owned sets used them very little.

Willie Chandler was thirty-two; he was tall and lanky and wore shell-rimmed glasses. He had a cheerful smile and people liked him and gave him what repair business they had, but it just wasn't enough to let him support himself and an invalid mother.

He had been born and raised in Bartlesville. His father had owned a not too prosperous feed business there and, after high school, he had worked in his father's store until his father's death.

But he had never liked the feed business, and had always been interested in radio; he had made his own sets as a boy and understood a little, at least, of how they worked. He had talked his mother into selling the feed store – the only valuable part of his father's estate – and using part of the proceeds to send him to Chicago for four months to attend a technical school that taught radio and television repairing. His mother had not been an invalid then, so it had been all right for him to leave her that long. At the end of the course, most of the rest of his father's money had gone into setting him up in business as a repairman.

The shop had never actually lost money, but it had earned pitifully little. A year later his mother had been partly paralysed by a stroke, and doctor and hospital bills had taken the rest of her money. He had to borrow several times from the bank and to stretch his credit to the breaking point with wholesalers to keep up his stock of tubes and other parts. Currently the shop brought him in barely enough to stave off foreclosure by paying interest on his loans, and to provide the absolute necessities of life for his mother and himself. At their home, a small rented cottage with the rent usually a month or two overdue, a neighbour came in to feed Mrs Chandler at lunchtime; Willie did all the rest of the work himself.

Except for his mother, whom he could not leave and who was unable to travel, he knew he'd be much better off to let the bank and his creditors foreclose and take his stock and equipment. In a city such as Milwaukee or Minneapolis, he could get a job as assistant in a repair shop big enough to use more than one man and make more money than he was making now, a lot more. But unless her condition should improve, and that seemed unlikely, he was stuck with the status quo. He couldn't even call the deal off and take a job in some other store in town, selling groceries or hardware or whatever, since there weren't any such jobs open. He'd even talked to the man who'd bought the feed store and had learned that there was no chance of his getting back the job he'd had with his father. He knew nothing of farming, and even if he could get a job as a farmhand he wouldn't make enough to take care of his mother in town; a good part of a farmhand's wages were in the form of room and board.

He was stuck with doing the best he could with what he had, at least until some day his mother got well or— He loved his mother too much to think about the 'or'.

He left the bleak view from his front window and went back to his workbench. He cleared space on it and opened the lunch he'd put up for himself that morning. Wrapped with a small thermos jar of hot coffee, there were two sandwiches. One was peanut butter and the other jelly; he'd been having to watch pennies for so long that he was used to such fare. Only on special occasions did he splurge on buying sandwich meat for a lunch. At home they seldom had meat other than hamburger, the cheapest kind, or a soup bone. Rent, both for the house and for the store, came first, and while he and his mother got enough to eat in quantity, it was seldom they could afford really good eating. The last really good eating he could remember had been for a month about three months ago when Walter Schroeder had been short of cash to pay for repairs to his television set and had offered him a smoked ham instead. It had been a twenty-pound ham and a real bargain for him, because he'd only replaced a couple of small tubes in the set and wouldn't have charged Schroeder more than six dollars in cash. The ham had been worth twice that and they'd eaten well for almost a month.

He finished the peanut butter sandwich and most of the jelly one and was finishing the hot coffee when he heard a scratching sound and looked around to see where it came from.

A cat was sitting on the sill of the side window, scratching at the glass with one paw. It was a big black cat and it looked as wet and bedraggled as though it had been in swimming. He walked over to the window and looked at the cat at closer range. He didn't recognise it as any cat he'd seen before. 'Well, what do you want, cat?' he asked it. He liked cats.

This one looked gaunt and almost starved – although he realised that part of the reason for its looking that way was that the rain had plastered down its fur. As though in answer to his question the cat opened its mouth and probably miaouwed, although he couldn't hear the miaouw through the glass, and then it pawed and scratched again at the pane.

'Want to come in out of the rain? Sensible cat!' Willie opened the window and the cat dropped down lightly on the floor.

He closed the window and looked down at the cat. 'Hungry?' he asked. ' 'Fraid all I can offer you is bread crusts with a little jelly, and that's not exactly cat food, but if you're really hungry—'

He sat down at the workbench again and broke a cat-sized piece off one of the crusts of the jelly sandwich. The cat sniffed at first, as though puzzled, and then ate the bit of crust. What was left of the crusts followed, in small pieces. Willie knew enough about cats to know that they would eat things handed to them in bite-sized pieces which they would ignore if offered in bulk.

'Thirsty too?' Willie asked. He rummaged about the junk on the workbench until he found a tin lid that would hold water. He took it to the sink at the back and filled it, and put it down. 'Sorry it isn't milk,' he said, 'but if you're thirsty enough—'

The cat took a few laps of the water. Willie looked at the two towels hanging over the sink. One of them was dirty enough to take home and wash, the next time he did washing. He took it down, 'Rubdown's the only other thing I can do for you, cat. I can't get you dry, but I can get you less wet than you are now.'

The cat held still and seemed to enjoy the rubbing. Willie

had barely finished when the phone rang. He answered it, 'Willie Chandler, radio and TV repairs.'

'This is Cap Hayden, Willie.' Cap Hayden ran the general store and was postmaster on the side. 'Asked me to call you when a package came from Chicago. It's here.'

'Swell, Cap. I'll be right over.'

'Just a second, Willie. Bring some money with you. It's COD, six dollars and eighty cents. And I can't put that on your bill 'cause it's government money for the post office department and I got to keep those things straight, in cash.'

'Damn it,' Willie said. 'Listen, the reason I'm in a hurry for that package is that one tube in it, a kind I didn't have in stock, is for Dolf Marsh's TV set. I've put a lot of work in it already but I can't finish it without that one tube. I'll get twenty bucks for the job – put in plenty of time on it – and he pays cash on the barrelhead, so I won't have to wait. But I've got only three dollars and some change in cash. If you can lend me the difference – out of your pocket, not putting it on the bill – I'll pay you the minute Dolf pays me.'

'Well – this one time, Willie. But like you said, in cash and you pay me when Dolf pays you.'

'Thanks a lot, Cap. Seeing you.'

Willie took his coat and hat from a hook on the wall, went to the door and turned. 'Cat,' he said, 'you keep shop while I'm gone. I won't bother locking up, nothing worth stealing. If anyone comes in – but nobody will – tell 'em to wait, that I'll be right back.'

He opened the door and then turned back again. 'Cat,' he said, 'let's get one thing straight. You're welcome to stay here till it's through raining and till you're fully dry. But I can't keep you. Ashamed as I am to admit it, I can't afford to keep a cat, here or at home. If you heard that phone conversation, you know how broke I am. I hope you got a home to go back to, because I wouldn't keep a cat unless I could feed it right – cat food and milk. And while that wouldn't run to much, not much is too much in my case, right now and for maybe a long time to come.'

The cat didn't answer and Willie went out and closed the door behind him. He ran to the general store and post office and, after getting his package, ran back again. He kept close to the buildings and didn't get wet enough for the rain to have soaked through his coat. He hung the coat and his hat up again and then went to his workbench to open the package.

The cat had been up on the bench and had jumped down when he opened the door. Now, in the film of dust which covered most of the bench he saw tracks which showed that it had wandered about quite a bit up there. It had apparently examined and sniffed at two television-set chassis – the one he was going to work on now that he had the needed vacuum tube; and another that needed a new picture tube for which he had also sent away. And the cat had apparently examined various odd parts and tools that had been lying loose.

Also there had been a loose-leaf handbook of circuits lying open at the back of the bench; and now it was open at a different page than the one he remembered. He said, 'Cat, you been studying electronics?' and grinned down at it, amused at the thought. He'd thought he'd left the book open at the circuit for Dolf Marsh's set, but he must have been wrong about that.

He opened the package, threw the cardboard away, and put the various small items of its contents where they belonged, keeping out the tube for Dolf's set and pulling its chassis along the bench in front of him.

He patted the edge of the bench invitingly and said, 'Come on, jump up again and watch me work. I don't mind teaching you electronics, except I don't know too much about it myself. Not the theory of it, that is. I just had a four months course. I can follow a circuit all right, but I don't know why it works any more than you do. But come on up.'

He patted the edge of the workbench again and this time the cat jumped up. It sat still, curled up and watching him with the intentness and alertness with which only a cat can watch something.

He was lonesome and he talked to it while he worked. He seemed to feel its sympathy, or thought he did, when after he had replaced the faulty tube and plugged in the set, he found that it still didn't work properly. He told the cat what he was doing while he checked condensers and capacitances, and looked for loose connections.

And then, having found the perfect audience he found himself telling it his personal problems, his worries about the shop and whether he could keep it going, his worries about his mother, about his doubtful future. He could relieve his mind, he found, by telling the cat things he couldn't possibly tell to any human being; not to his mother, because they would cause her more worry and grief than she already had; not to anyone else, because to no one else could he admit how hopeless his prospects looked to him – let alone how much he wanted to get married, but couldn't see even dating a girl, under the circumstances. Even taking one to a movie would have taken money he could not afford from his slim budget.

The cat was a good listener. When finally it jumped down from the bench and ran to the door, where it miaouwed and pawed at the glass, he walked to the door reluctantly to let it out.

'Cat,' he said. 'Come back any time. Same window, same signal. I'll share my lunch with you if I can't do anything more.'

The rain had stopped. He watched the cat through the glass of the door as it ran across the street and disappeared into an alleyway.

Obviously it had a home somewhere. But, he thought,

some day he'd have to get a cat of his own. It couldn't cost him much to feed one, and it would be the first extravagance he'd allow himself, if and when the pressure on him ever eased off a little.

He never knew, never suspected, that he had just been judged and found wanting; that he had been spared an experience which would have led soon to an early death.

CHAPTER TWELVE

Doc Staunton had spent the morning making voluminous notes on the two human suicides and the phenomena which seemed to have accompanied them – at least in regard to time and place, if no other connection could be traced. But he wanted more than notes; while statements at the inquest and conversations, especially the ones at the Gross farm, were so fresh in his mind he wanted them down on paper, as nearly verbatim as he could get them down.

But getting *everything* down, he realised, was going to be one hell of a job, especially as he didn't have a typewriter with him and was only a mediocre typist in any case. He spent half an hour writing in longhand and had only three pages, giving a detailed description of the manner of death of the dog and just a start into the inquest testimony of Charlotte Garner, when he began to get writer's cramp. It was going to take him thirty to fifty pages, he realised, to get all the facts down in detail, let alone his deductions, his mental processes which refused to permit him to accept the allied phenomena – the apparently suicidal animal deaths and missing soup stock and gravy from Mrs Gross's kitchen – as simply isolated and coincidental happenings having nothing to do with the human deaths. It would be almost as bad as writing a book in longhand.

But it had to be put down, somehow, while it was fresh in his mind. He considered going into Green Bay to try to rent a tape recorder, or to buy one if he couldn't rent one. But he hated the things, mostly because he liked to be able to pace while he dictated. And in any case he'd have to hire someone to transcribe the tapes, so it would be better to find a stenographer who could take his dictation in shorthand and transcribe it.

Probably he'd have to find someone in Green Bay, but he'd try Bartlesville first on his way through it.

The editor of the *Clarion*, Bartlesville's weekly newspaper, would be his best source of information. And Doc knew him because by now he'd played in two poker games with him. Yes, Ed Hollis would be the best person to ask. He might even know someone in Wilcox, which was a little bigger than Bartlesville and only about half as far as Green Bay.

Hollis was pounding an ancient Underwood when Doc walked in just before noon. He said, 'Just a second, Doc,' and finished a sentence before he looked up. 'What gives? And are you playing in the game tonight? Hans just phoned me that there's one on – and there's no way of reaching you by phone. Lucky you dropped in, if you want to take some more of our money.'

'I'll try to make it, Ed. But I dropped in to ask you something. Is there anyone in town here who can take shorthand and do typing?'

'Sure. Miss Talley, Miss Amanda Talley.'

'Is she working now? Would I have to use her evenings?'

'She isn't working now, except an occasional part-time job. She's an English teacher at the high school. Summers – except for a short vacation, and she's already taken one this year – she stays in town and takes any small jobs like that she can get. Bookkeeping too. When a merchant here gets his books in a mess she can straighten them out for him. Things like that.'

'She fast at taking shorthand?'

'She is,' Ed said. 'I've used her a time or two myself when I've got behind on something. Used to teach shorthand, typing, bookkeeping at a business college before she got into high school teaching. That was a long time ago, but she's kept up on it. She's been trying to get the county board to let her teach commercial classes in the high school here, but she hasn't got anywhere with them yet. Me, I'm for it, and I've run editorials saying so. Why make the kids here go to Green Bay or Milwaukee after high school and pay for a commercial course, if one can be given free here? Do 'em more good than a lot of other subjects they have to study.'

'Sounds ideal,' Doc said. 'If she teaches English, she can probably even spell. But do you know if she's free now?'

'I can find out.' Ed Hollis reached for the phone, but stopped before he picked it up. 'How much of a job will it be? An hour or a week or what?'

Doc said, 'I'd guess about four hours' dictation, give or take an hour. And then a day or two to transcribe it on a typewriter.'

Hollis nodded and picked up the phone. He asked for a number and got it. 'Miss Talley? Friend of mine here's got a couple of days' work, typing and shorthand. Can you do it for him? . . . Fine. Just a second.'

He held his hand over the mouthpiece and looked up at Doc. 'Says she can start whenever you want her. But it's practically noon now. Shall I tell her you'll see her around one o'clock? I can tell you how to get there; it's only a few blocks.'

'Excellent.'

Hollis spoke into the phone again. Right, Miss Talley. He'll see you somewhere around one o'clock. His name's Doc Staunton . . . Okay. 'Bye now.'

He looked up at Doc again. 'She reminded me to tell you her rates.' He grinned. 'Guess she thought they might scare you. Ten bucks a day. Or buck and a half an hour for shorter jobs.'

'Reasonable as hell. Have lunch with me, Ed, to help me kill time till one?'

'Wish I could, but I've got about an hour's work and then I'm knocking off for the day. Rather get it over with first, and then go home. Just phoned the missus I'd be home between one and half past and to hold lunch.'

He gave Doc Miss Talley's address and then walked to the door with him and showed him how to get to the place.

When Doc got there at one o'clock, he found it a neat, well-kept little cottage. Matching it in size was a little Volkswagen in the driveway beside it.

Miss Talley, when she answered his knock at the door, proved not to be equivalently small, at least vertically. She was almost a head taller than Doc, albeit so slender that their weight was probably just about the same. She could have been anywhere from fifty-five to sixty-five, and probably, Doc decided, was just about halfway between. She wore steel-rimmed spectacles and was dressed neatly and conservatively in grey that just matched her hair, which she wore in a tight bun at the back of her neck.

Add a frumpy hat and an umbrella, Doc thought, and she'd exactly fit his mental picture of Stuart Palmer's female detective character, Hildegarde Withers. But she looked competent and, after all, he wasn't hiring her as a party girl.

'Dr Saunders?' And when he nodded, she stepped back. 'Won't you come in?'

Doc said, 'Thank you, Miss Talley,' and entered.

'If you'll be seated, Doctor, I'll get my notebook and—'

'Uh – Miss Talley. I suppose I *can* dictate here, but I think I'd be distracted and I could do a lot better at my own place. It's about eight miles out of town, last house on what they call the Bascombe Road. If you could possibly work out there – for taking the dictation, that is; it will be perfectly all right if you do the typing back here. The only thing is that I'm staying there alone and—' He floundered.

Miss Talley smiled slightly. 'We're alone here, Doctor, so that shouldn't matter. I assure you that I don't feel the need of a chaperone. Or rather, I'm one myself, I chaperone most of the high school dances and socials. Of course the time involved in travelling—'

'Naturally,' Doc said. 'We're punching the time clock as of now, one p.m. If you'll get your notebook and pencils—'

Outside, Miss Talley insisted that she wanted to take her own car, the Volkswagen, and follow him out instead of riding with him. She took as a polite lie (which it was) his statement that he had to come back to town anyway at the end of the afternoon so it would be no inconvenience for him to take her out and bring her back, but he finally convinced her; she got into the station wagon with him.

The quiet, stealthy little cats. Such wonderful hosts, with their soft padded feet, their quickness, their keen hearing. Able to go almost anywhere and to be taken for granted, not noticed.

With several of them – one at a time, of course – the mind thing had visited every farm between the Gross farm and town, except two that had fierce dogs that stayed around the barnyard; one of them had killed the cat-host in use at the time.

But it didn't seem to matter that he'd had to skip two of the farms; he'd learned nothing of importance at the other ones. He had started to make a survey of the town itself next, starting with the person who logically should have been his best bet as an electronics expert, the local television repairman, but he had proved utterly hopeless as a host, if for no other reason than that he was too tied down for financial reasons.

The big black cat that had shared Willie Chandler's lunch and then had left him spent the remainder of the afternoon exploring the rest of the town and listening to conversations here and there without learning much worth knowing; it spent the evening similarly until the mind thing remembered the interesting little man called Staunton who had visited the Gross farm with the sheriff, and who had been so interested in the suicide of Siegfried Gross. He decided to let the rest of the town go until he had found and investigated the man called Staunton.

And he must live, the mind thing decided, out farther from town than the Grosses, and on the same road. In the body of a sparrow, the mind thing had flown to the road to try to follow Staunton and had seen two cars moving away, in opposite directions, both too distant for him to catch up with or follow. Since it would have been much more likely that the sheriff would have been driving into Bartlesville, and through it to his office in Wilcox, Staunton must have been going in the opposite direction, away from town.

There were only fifteen or sixteen more farmhouses in that direction before the road ended, and he decided to investigate them the first thing in the morning, before finishing his check of the town.

He started the black cat out of town, but when it was only about halfway along the road it fell; he realised that he had overworked it and made it travel too fast. Not only was it in a state of utter exhaustion, but its feet were bleeding, leaving a noticeable trail. Even a night's rest, the mind thing realised, wouldn't restore it enough to make it a good host for another day. He forced the cat to get to its feet and stay that way, to leave the road and turn across fields till it dropped dead of exhaustion within less than half a mile.

Early the next morning he took another host, a small grey cat that lived, with several other cats, on the third farm east from the Gross farm, towards the end of the road. He checked its memories first; luckily, it was a cat that had done exploring and from its mental pictures of the occupants of nearby farmhouses the mind thing was able to eliminate five of them, besides the farm on which the grey cat lived, as places where Staunton might be. These five farms included the ones between the Gross farm and the cat's own home farm, so he was able to start it directly east and skip the next three farms.

From there he checked each house carefully, staying as near the road as he could so he would not miss Staunton if Staunton should drive into town and pass him.

That is just what happened a little after eleven o'clock, when he was moving across a field between two farms, but near the edge of the road. He heard a noisy car coming from the east and hurried to the open in time to see an old station wagon pass on the way into town. The man Staunton was driving it.

At the next farm the grey cat was treed atop a small shed for almost an hour by a dog until the woman of the house, annoyed by the barking, came out and called in the dog. By now the mind thing, correlating many things, including Tommy Hoffman's memories, was sure that Staunton had come from the last house. Staunton, from his appearance and from his way of talking at the time he had been at the Gross house, was almost certainly not a farmer, and only the last house on this road was not being farmed. Someone in the East, Tommy had known vaguely, had bought it and lived in it only a month or two each year, using it as a base for fishing and relative seclusion. Almost certainly, Staunton would be living there.

He inspected the next two farms only casually and came to the last house.

Yes, here were recent tyre tracks in the yard – where Staunton apparently kept his car, since there was no garage – and other signs of recent occupancy. But had Staunton left permanently?

Luckily there seemed to be no dog on the premises, so the cat was able to examine the house closely and at leisure.

There were several cellar windows at ground level and through them he was able to hear the throbbing of a gasoline generator and the hum of an electric motor. That meant Staunton had not left permanently, and would be back. But was he living here alone, or had he left someone behind him in the house?

The cat made a full circuit of the house, looking for a way in. There was none. Several of the downstairs windows were open, but only an inch or two. Only one upstairs window was open wide.

The mind thing realised he would have to wait till Staunton came back to investigate further. But that might not be until late afternoon or evening, so he looked over the surrounding area. Keeping out of sight most of the time, in case someone was in the house, he made several circuits of the yard. The only building aside from the house was a small wooden one that had probably served as a tool shed, but the door was gone and the shed was empty. There were signs of what had once been the foundation for a barn, but the barn was long gone; either it had burned or had been razed for its lumber.

He went close to the house again, this time pausing under each window to listen for the sound of voices or of someone moving inside, but he heard nothing.

He walked over to where the cleared area of the yard ended in clumps of weeds and lay down behind one of them to wait. He let his host sleep; there was, he'd realized after what he'd done to the black cat, no advantage in pushing a host beyond its capacity and having to get a new one for each operation. And he knew it would awaken instantly at the sound of an approaching car.

The wait wasn't as long as he'd feared it might be. The cat had been sleeping only half an hour when its sensitive ears told the mind thing that a car was turning into the yard. He opened his host's eyes and moved to peer through the weeds.

It was Staunton's station wagon, and Staunton was driving it, but there was a woman with him. A tall, thin, elderly woman.

The mind thing knew her – from Tommy Hoffman's memories, which he had made his own. She was Miss Talley, and she had been Tommy Hoffman's high school English teacher. (Tally Ho, the students used to call her, among themselves.) Was she a friend of Staunton's? Was he another teacher? Then he saw that she carried a shorthand notebook and remembered that she sometimes supplemented her income by doing stenographic or bookkeeping work outside of school hours and during vacations. That, then, must be Staunton's reason for bringing her here. That was good; if he was going to dictate letters to her, the mind thing could learn plenty about Staunton by listening to those letters.

The moment they had gone inside, he ran to the house and around it, so close that he could not be seen from the inside, pausing briefly to listen under each window to find out what room they were in. He heard them – their voices, but not the words – from under a window at the back, probably a kitchen window. He crouched under it to leap up on to the window sill, as he had done at the other houses. From there he'd be able to hear everything said. And if he was seen, nothing would be thought of it, as he now knew by experience. Possibly if they were people who liked cats, they might even open the window and ask him in, as Willie Chandler had done. That would be even better.

He tried the jump and found to his annoyance that he was short by a full eight inches even of getting his host's front paws on the window ledge. The damned cat was too small. Any one of the fully grown cats that had been former hosts could have reached that ledge easily. For a moment he considered getting rid of his current host as quickly as he could kill it and trying for another – but the new one might be miles away, too far to bring here before Staunton had finished his dictating. He must keep that as a last desperate resort if everything else failed.

Quickly he ran to the back door, which would also open into the kitchen, put the cat's ear against it; the door was too thick; again he could hear voices but not words.

Around the house. Still the one upstairs window was the only one open wider than an inch or two. But he saw something now that he had not noticed before. There was a tree, an elm, at that side of the house, and one of its branches dipped near the open window, the tip of the branch about four feet above the sill. The branch tapered considerably; possibly the cat's weight would bend it down to a point from which he could jump to the window sill.

Quickly the grey cat climbed the tree and worked its way warily along the branch. Yes, as it neared the end, the branch bent; his jump from the end of it wouldn't be too difficult. But first, he looked into the room – it was a bedroom – and made sure that the door to it was open. It would have done him no good at all to get in, only to find himself blocked by a closed bedroom door.

He jumped. Then from the window sill he looked back and saw that, as he had suspected, it would not also serve him as an exit. The branch had sprung back and it was too far away from him to jump to it from the window. But other ways out would no doubt present themselves; Staunton wouldn't keep all the downstairs windows closed or almost closed all of the time.

He ran out into the hallway and down the stairs, and then quietly padded along the hallway that led from the front doorway to the kitchen. He stopped just short of the turn in the passage; it was a perfect listening post.

There was the sound of a refrigerator door opening, and now he could hear the words that were spoken.

CHAPTER THIRTEEN

'Are you sure you won't have a beer with me, Miss Talley?' Doc asked. 'Dictating is dry work, and taking it down must be even drier.'

Miss Talley smiled slightly, the first time Doc had seen her do so. 'If you insist, Doctor. But you must promise to keep it a deep secret. In towns as small as this one, teachers simply do not drink or smoke.'

'I'll keep your secret,' Doc said over his shoulder as he took a second can of beer from the refrigerator. 'I wish I could tempt you to smoke too, but alas, I have only pipes to offer. Uh – it won't bother you if I smoke while I'm dictating, will it?'

'Not at all. I rather like the smell of pipe smoke, except possibly in very confined quarters. And this is a magnificently large kitchen you have.'

'The better to pace in. I like it; I practically live in it. Except when I'm out fishing or in town.' He came back with two glasses of beer, put one in front of Miss Talley and the other across the table from it. He sat down. 'You can put down that pencil, Miss Talley,' he said. 'I'm too lazy to start dictating this minute. Unless you'd rather have me dictate than listen to me talk. Sometimes I think my students would rather have me hew to the line more than I do.'

'Your students? Are you a teacher too, Doctor?'

'Yes, Miss Talley. Physics, at MIT. I specialise in electronics and, though to a lesser degree, in nuclear physics.'

Miss Talley had put down her pencil; she stared at him. 'Staunton – Dr Ralph S. Staunton? Of course. And you've worked on all the big satellite projects.'

Doc smiled. 'Not quite all. But I'm really flattered, Miss Talley, that you've heard of me. Are you interested in science?'

'Of course I am. Who isn't? Especially when it comes to matters of reaching the moon and the planets. I've been an avid reader of science fiction for a great many years.'

'*You*, Miss Talley?'

'Of course. Why not?'

Why not indeed, Doc thought, feeling himself backed into a corner. He could hardly tell her that she had looked to him to be just about the least likely person to be an avid reader of science fiction, so he decided he'd best treat the 'Why not?' as a rhetorical question. He said, 'I'm afraid I do my escape reading in the form of mystery novels. I know some scientists do read science fiction and enjoy it, but when I read for relaxation I like to get as far away from science as I can.'

'I can understand that,' Miss Talley said. 'Is what you're going to dictate now scientific matter, or are you just catching up on correspondence?'

'Not either – and I'm afraid it's difficult to explain just what I am doing. But something strange has been going on near here. I've been – well, investigating a bit, and I want to put what I've learned thus far down in the form of a statement of my investigation to date, before I might forget a point or two.'

Miss Talley stared at him. 'You mean – the suicides?'

'Yes. Don't tell me they've aroused your curiosity too? I thought everyone around here, from the sheriff down, took them as perfectly ordinary events.'

'Not quite, Doctor. Incidentally, I know now where I saw you before – at the inquest on Tommy Hoffman. You must have been at the back; I passed you on my way out.'

Doc filled his pipe and started to tamp it down. 'I was there. I didn't see you, that I recall, but that's because I was trying to keep my eye on Mr Garner and reach him before he got away. I didn't succeed, but talked to the sheriff instead.'

'You mean you had further information on something connected with— Oh, never mind answering that, Doctor. If it's anything connected with Tommy's suicide, I'll learn about it while you're dictating; there's no need for you to say it twice.'

Doc waited till he finished lighting his pipe before answering. 'That makes sense, Miss Talley. But you say you've been interested too, so I'm going to ask what you know first. If you have any relevant facts that I don't already have, I might as well learn them before I start so I can add them to what I do know. Now, on Tommy Hoffman, do you know anything at all that didn't come out at the inquest?'

'Not facts exactly, but I knew Tommy. Charlotte, too, for that matter. I taught them both freshman English and had them in a class of mine in great English literature again last year. And I know that Tommy was as sane a boy as I've ever known. Not bright and not much of a scholar, but sane, ordinary, and uncomplicated. And perfectly sound physically. I talked to Dr Gruen – he delivered Tommy and was his doctor all of his life – and he tells me that Tommy was in perfect physical shape. Measles and whooping cough, both years ago, were the only illnesses he ever had.'

'But that could mean the doctor hadn't seen him for quite a few years.'

'It could, but as it happens it doesn't. Tommy was injured playing high school baseball last spring. No, not a head injury; it was a broken rib. Dr Gruen treated it. And our school has a strict rule, a very good one I believe, requiring that when a student is injured in any athletic contest he must have a thorough physical examination before his readmittance to the team. Dr Gruen told me, when I asked him last week, that when he examined Tommy only about two months ago he was absolutely sound and in perfect health. *Mens sana in corpore sano.* I can guarantee the mental part; literally or figuratively, he didn't know what a neurosis is.'

'Nor apparently,' said Doc dryly, 'was he suffering from sexual repression. What do you know about Charlotte Garner?'

'A good girl – and I mean that; I'm not a prude, Doctor, despite my age and occupation. And a smart girl, a little smarter than Tommy was. Even smart enough never to have let him suspect she was the smarter of the two.'

'Imaginative?'

'No, very literal, Doctor. If you're thinking about her story about the field mouse, it would have happened just as she described it, not exaggerated in the slightest. And I admire her courage for having managed to bring it out at the inquest, despite the coroner and the sheriff both pooh-poohing it as irrelevant when they talked to her before the inquest. I don't know how it might *not* be irrelevant, but it's too – too bizarre an episode to be brushed off when it occurred in connection with as bizarre a suicide as that of Tommy.'

'I agree with you, Miss Talley. Anything else you can tell me? Aside from what was brought out at the inquest, of course.'

'I'm afraid not. And I know very little about the suicide of Mr Gross. I mentioned "two suicides" simply because of the coincidence of two suicides so close together, in time and in location, when we hadn't had a suicide closer than Wilcox for years, and when there could be no possible connection between them. I mean, Tommy must have known Gross by sight and possibly vice versa, but they wouldn't really have known each other.'

Doc smiled and tamped his pipe to relight it. 'What would you say, Miss Talley, to *six* suicides, two human and four animal, starting with that of the field mouse, which apparently forced Tommy to kill it by attacking him? What would you say to the apparent suicides of the mouse and a dog – the Hoffman dog – in connection with that of Tommy Hoffman? And the apparent suicides of an owl and a cat – the Gross cat – in connection with that of Siegfried Gross? Not to mention the minor mystery – or *is* it minor? – of the disappearance from Mrs Gross's refrigerator, on the night her husband killed himself, of a quart of soup stock and a bowl of gravy?'

Miss Talley's eyes were wide, her face pale with – with what? Doc studied it and decided that it was excitement, not fear.

She said very quietly, 'Dr Staunton, if you're not – if those things are true, you'd better start dictating before I explode with curiosity.' She picked up her pencil, opened the shorthand notebook.

Doc lighted his pipe again and started pacing and dictating. Not steadily, of course; sometimes there were minutes between sentences, since he wanted everything in sequence and in detail, coldly factual and without sensationalism or exaggeration. It took him an hour and a half, making the time a few minutes after three o'clock, to finish his description of the first three deaths and the negative rabies report from the laboratory in Green Bay.

He sat down across from Miss Talley and knocked out his pipe, which he'd refilled twice and relighted at least a score of times during his pacing. 'Think we'd better rest a few minutes before I tackle the Gross case,' he said. 'I must have walked a good two miles and you must be getting writer's cramp.'

Miss Talley shook her head. 'I'm not, but I suppose you do deserve a rest. We're just getting to the really new part for me. I knew everything about Tommy, up to the point where you ran over the dog. Almost everything about Mr Gross will be new to me.'

'Give me ten minutes, Miss Talley. And meanwhile shall we have another glass of beer?'

Miss Talley demurred at first, but let him talk her into it.

After their first sips, she asked, 'How many copies of this will you want?'

'Three,' Doc said. 'One for myself and two I'm going to send to friends of mine for their opinions. One is a top research physician; I'm going to ask him if there's any possibility of the existence of a rare disease communicable, as is rabies, from animal to man and vice versa, which could lead to insanity and suicidal behaviour. The other friend is an excellent mathematician; his speciality is symbolic logic, but he knows actuarial math too, and has cracked some pretty tough problems in it. I want him to quote me the odds on this series of events being coincidental as against interconnected. Later, probably not today, I'll dictate a letter to each of them to go with his copy of the statement.'

'Would you mind if I make an extra copy for myself, Doctor?'

'Not at all, Miss Talley.'

She smiled. 'Wonderful. I would have made myself a copy anyway, but it's nicer to be able to do it with permission.'

Doc laughed. He was finding Miss Talley's wide-open mind and curiosity very stimulating, after his failure to be able to convince the sheriff that his investigation, if one could call it that, wasn't even scratching the surface of events. And he liked her honesty in admitting she'd have made herself a copy even without his permission. In fact, he liked Miss Talley.

He was even beginning to think of propositioning her. His department's budget at MIT had been increased for next year to include provision, for the first time, for a full-time secretary and record clerk. If he could get her in on his recommendation she'd be ideal for the job. It would pay at least as much as she could be making here and she was certainly wasted in teaching high school English in a small town. But he'd wait a while and be sure before mentioning the possibility to her. There was no hurry.

When their beer was finished Doc started pacing and dictating again. He finished the job at half past four, said, 'That's all, Miss Tally,' and sank into the chair. 'Give me a few minutes to rest and I'll drive you home.'

'You mean that's all? Or that all for today? I thought you were going to go into your deductions from the facts.'

'I've changed my mind,' Doc said. 'For one thing, I don't know what my deductions are, not surely enough to put them down. Besides, for the purpose for which I intend this, it would be wrong for me to draw conclusions. The two friends I mentioned, the medico and the mathematician, should have just the facts and draw their own conclusions without being influenced by mine, such as they are. Miss Talley, I have only wild ideas – and I can't believe any of them.'

'I see your point. But it shouldn't take you long to dictate the two covering letters, should it? Why not get them out of the way today, so when I turn over the statements to you the letters will be with them, and you can mail them right away?'

'It makes sense, but I'm afraid I'm just not up to giving any more dictation today. Tell you what – when I drop around to your place to pick up the statements I'll dictate the two letters. They won't be long and you can type them while I'm reading over what I've just dictated, for any corrections. And if you'll address envelopes too, I can mail them while I'm in town. Will that be all right?'

'That will be fine.' Miss Talley leafed back quickly through her notebook to see how many pages she had filled.

'I think this is just about two full days' typing. And today is Tuesday. I think I can promise to have this ready for you any time after noon on Thursday, if I work evenings too.'

'Do you usually work evenings?'

'Ordinarily I don't. But this isn't *work* – and I'm not going to take any pay for it, so that makes it different. Doctor, having the opportunity to do this is the most exciting and fascinating thing that's ever happened to me. And I don't need the money. So if you're going to insist on paying me, you've wasted an afternoon. I'll type myself a copy from these notes, but you'll have to dictate them all over to someone else for your copies.'

Doc sighed. He realized that she meant what she said and that there was no use in arguing. His only recourse would be to send her a present from Boston after he was back there so she couldn't refuse it. Unless, of course, she did want and could get the secretarial job he had in mind for her there; in that case he'd make it up to her some other way.

'Very well, Miss Talley. But that makes you my partner in this, and I may ask you to do even more.'

'I'll be glad to. What did you have in mind?'

'You might keep your ear to the ground for a while, in town. I usually get in once a day – at least since I got interested the day of the Hoffman boy's inquest – so if anything important happens I'll hear about it without too much delay, as I heard about the Gross suicide a few days ago. But, short of another human death, something interesting might happen without my hearing of it, something not necessarily spectacular in itself but that just might fit in with whatever I – I mean we – are investigating. You know as much as I do now, so your judgement would be as good as mine as to what might be worth reporting.'

'I'll be more than glad to do that. But how shall I get in touch with you if I learn anything? You don't have a telephone this far out, do you?'

'No, I haven't. And now I'm sorry for the first time. But the one place I invariably go in town is the post office, to pick up my mail, if any. If you leave a message with the postmaster for me to phone you I'll be sure to get it. Well, everything's settled then and I'll see you early Thursday afternoon at your place. I'm rested now. Are you ready?'

She put notebook and pencil in her handbag and they left by the front door and went to the station wagon. Doc started the engine and threw the car into gear; he was just about to release the clutch when Miss Talley said, 'Oh, I was going to ask you to introduce me to your cat, but I forgot. It doesn't matter.'

Doc kept his foot on the clutch pedal and turned to her. 'Cat?' he said. 'Miss Talley, I don't have a cat. Do you mean you saw one in the house?'

'I – why, I thought I did. I was sure at the time, but—'

Doc put the shift lever back in neutral and turned off the ignition. 'Must be a stray cat that got in somehow,' he said. 'If you don't mind waiting, I'll check. Might as well let it out so it can go home, if it's got a home.'

He got out of the car and let himself back into the house, closing the door behind him. He made a quick round of the lower floor, seeing no cat. Nor any open window through which a cat could have come and left. Several windows were open an inch or two, but none wide enough for a cat larger than a small kitten to get through – and besides, a kitten couldn't jump up to a window ledge. The cellar door was closed and had been that way all day. He went upstairs. Again no cat was in sight, although he didn't look under beds or behind the bathtub or other possible hiding places. The only window open upstairs was in the bedroom he slept in.

He went to the open window and looked out speculatively at a tree branch that came close to it, but considerably above the level of the sill. He leaned out and tugged lightly at the end of the branch; it bent downward easily. Yes, even a small cat's weight could bend the branch down so it might be able to jump to the window sill. But it could never get out that way. Nor, he decided, after looking down, by jumping down. On to soft grass, just possibly, but the ground under the window was hard-baked and stone-studded. A cat jumping that far to such a surface would be, if not killed, too seriously injured to be able to get away.

But it came to him suddenly that a cat, if there was one in the house, just might want to die; the Gross's cat had seemed to want to be killed, and the other animals—

He closed the window, went downstairs and left the house. If there was a cat inside now, it would still be there when he got back and he'd worry about it then.

He got back in the car, started it, and backed it around. 'I didn't see a cat, Miss Talley,' he said. 'Are you sure you saw one? And just when and where?'

'I thought I was sure at the time, but I suppose it could have been a momentary optical illusion. It was while you were dictating; or rather, while you were pausing between sentences. I looked up, and saw, or thought I saw, the head of a cat sticking around the corner of the hallway passage leading to the kitchen alongside the stairs. I didn't say anything or call to it because I didn't want to interrupt your train of thought. Then you started dictating again, and when I looked that way again, it was gone.'

She paused a moment. 'Now that I think back, though, I'm sure I must have imagined seeing it. It was just a quick momentary glance and then I looked back at my notebook as you started talking. It's very easy to imagine something under those circumstances.'

'I suppose so,' Doc said, making his voice easier than he felt. 'Well, if I do find a cat there, I'll let you know.'

For a few minutes they rode in silence and then Miss Talley said, 'Doctor, you don't really believe there could be a

– a disease, a contagious disease, that could pass from man to animal and vice versa and – make its victims insanely suicidal?'

'I'll admit I've never heard of one, so it would have to be pretty rare.'

'Pretty rare – but pretty well known just *because* it would be so unusual. If it were known at all, one of us would certainly have heard or read of it somewhere, sometime.'

'I'm afraid that's rather probable. But, Miss Talley, aside from that possibility – or sheer coincidence – can you think of any other explanation?'

'Certainly I can. Don't you remember about the Gadarene swine, Doctor?'

CHAPTER FOURTEEN

'Gadarene swine . . .' Doc said musingly. 'They sound familiar, but I'm afraid I can't place them.'

'In the Bible,' Miss Talley said. 'Book of Luke, I think. Christ came upon a man who was possessed by devils, and ordered them to leave him. There was a herd of swine nearby. Let's see; I think I can quote the crucial verse: "Then went the devils out of the man, and entered into the swine: and the herd ran violently down a steep place into the lake, and were choked." '

Doc groaned softly. 'Miss Talley, don't tell me you believe in demoniac possession. Please.'

'Of course I don't. That is, I don't believe in demons. But possession—'

'Possession by what, then? I'm a materialist, Miss Talley. I'll admit that the Rhine experiments and some other things have shaken me just a little bit, enough so I don't dogmatically deny the possibility of wild talents like telepathy and telekinesis. And of course hypnosis and post-hypnotic suggestion are fully accepted scientifically. But not even the wildest enthusiast for parapsychology has suggested that one mind can take over another and control it from inside.'

'One *human* mind,' said Miss Talley firmly. 'There are billions of planets besides Earth in the universe, and millions of them must be inhabited. How do we know what capabilities and limitations a *non*-human mind might have? How do we know what an alien, an extra-terrestrial, might be able to do?'

'Hmmm,' said Doc. Wondering for a moment if Miss Talley was joking, he moved his head far enough to be able to see her face in the rear vision mirror. Her eyes looked excited, the rest of her face was calm.

She said, 'Aren't we working right now to get men on to other planets? What makes you think we're the most advanced race in the universe? How do you *know* there isn't an alien here?'

'Hmmm,' said Doc. 'I suppose I don't, but then again I don't know that there is. But why *an* alien, instead of aliens?'

'Because only one person or animal has been – I'll call it possessed, for lack of a better word – at a time. The field mouse, then Tommy after the field mouse was dead, the hound after Tommy was dead, the owl after the hound was dead, the cat— You see what I mean, Doctor. Never two at any one time. And that's why he makes his hosts commit suicide, so he can get his mind back out of them and be free to take a different host.'

Something seemed to prickle between Doc's shoulder blades. But he said, 'You certainly have an imagination, Miss Talley. Possibly I should read science fiction instead of mysteries.'

'Possibly you should. But with what's happening, possibly you won't have to, to have your imagination stimulated. If there *is* a cat at your place, maybe it's host to an alien who was spying on us. You might ask him.'

Doc laughed. 'And then kill the cat so the alien can take *me* over, eh? If that happens, I'll let you know, Miss Talley.'

But after he'd dropped her off at her little house, his expression was thoughtful and a little worried as he drove home. It was ridiculous, of course, but what if—?

He let himself in the door carefully, making sure nothing

got out past him. He saw nothing, heard nothing, out of the ordinary.

He leaned against the inside of the door, filled his pipe with tobacco and lighted it.

He went into the living-room and sat down in his favourite chair, a leather upholstered morris. Backed against the biggest window and with a lamp standing beside it, it afforded excellent light for reading either by day or by night. A paperback mystery novel lay open on one arm of the chair, but he didn't pick it up.

Should he search the house? It would be a long and tedious job to look everywhere a cat might hide. And besides, downstairs here an intelligent cat wouldn't even have to hide, since there was no door in the doorway between living-room and kitchen, or in the doorway between the kitchen and the hallway that led to the front door and back to the living-room again. It could simply move from room to room ahead of him and stay out of his sight that way. Right now it could be sitting in the kitchen. And if it heard him heading that way it could come back here by way of the hall – or through the kitchen-living-room door if he went by the hallway. It could move more silently than he could and would have better hearing.

That is if there was a cat.

And if there was, why shouldn't it be a perfectly ordinary cat, here for perfectly good catlike reasons? Well ... certainly it wasn't very usual for a cat to enter a house, without good reason at least, by making what must have been a fairly dangerous jump from a tree branch to an upstairs window. And another thing, why would it keep itself so well and thoroughly hidden for so long, all the time he'd been dictating?

His pipe had burned out and he knocked the dottle out of it and wondered if he should get himself something to eat, or drive into town for something. Somehow he didn't feel like making dinner for himself.

But the cat . . .?

Suddenly he thought of a way of telling, on return, whether or not there was a cat here in the house – at least, if it moved around and didn't stay hidden in one place. Along with the pots and pans in one of the cupboards there was a flour sifter; he'd used it a few times to flour fish when he was going to fry them. He got it now and put a little flour in it. Then he went to the foot of the stairs and over the bottom few steps scattered a thin, almost invisible film of flour, not turning the handle of the sifter but merely tapping the side of it lightly with one finger as he moved it. He did the same thing in the middle of the hallway, and at the doorway between the living-room and the kitchen.

Then, so he wouldn't have to walk through any of the cat-traps he had just set, he left by the back door and drove into town.

He ate at the place where he knew he'd be served by the most talkative waitress in town. She lived up to her billing – but there was no new suicide, nothing new in the form of strange actions of either wild or domestic animals. The most exciting thing that had happened in the past twenty-four hours had been a fire at Smalley's Feed Store; the damage had been slight and the cause had been traced to defective wiring.

No pigs had sprouted wings; no dogs had been seen climbing telephone poles. He'd asked about those points specifically, not so much to get a laugh – although he had – but because they'd make her remember if she had heard any stories about animals behaving unnaturally.

He was heading for his car when someone called out 'Hey Staunton.' It was Dr Gruen, and he came closer so he wouldn't have to yell the rest of what he had to say. 'Getting up a little poker game and we need one more sucker. How's about it?'

'Well,' Doc said, 'guess I can sit in an hour or two. Back room at the tavern?'

Gruen nodded. 'I'm going over to get Lem. We'll be starting in about fifteen minutes.'

'Good,' Doc said. 'Just time for me to get a spot of fortification at the bar. See you when you get there.'

Time can be subjective; a few minutes in a dentist's chair can be longer than a few hours in a good poker game. Doc played what he thought was a short time and suddenly realised, when they quit playing, that it was almost midnight. And also that he was hungry again; but both of the Bartlesville restaurants would be closed by now; he would have to wait till he got home and then make himself a sandwich.

At the house he parked his car in the yard and was almost at the door before he remembered that, unless Miss Talley had had a momentary hallucination, there was a cat in his house.

He let himself in by way of the kitchen door, being careful that nothing got past him. The moonlight was so bright that, until he closed the kitchen door, he could not possibly have missed seeing anything as large as a mouse. He heard no sound.

He flicked on the kitchen light and looked around. He remembered the flour he had sprinkled on the floor and walked over to the doorway.

There were cat tracks in the flour.

He called out, 'All right, Cat. Show yourself if you want anything to eat or drink. I'm not going to hunt for you, but you're not getting out of here till I've met you.'

He went to the refrigerator and opened it. He got out the necessary ingredients and made himself a ham sandwich and took it and a bottle of beer over to the table and sat down.

He did a lot of thinking while he ate the sandwich slowly

and sipped the beer. He didn't think he liked what he was thinking. He was frightened, without knowing what he was frightened about. He knew that he didn't want to turn out the kitchen lights and go upstairs to bed in the dark. Although he knew the house so well by now that he seldom used his flashlight, he got it from a cupboard drawer. He had it in his hand and turned it on when he flicked off the kitchen light.

He played it ahead of him as he went through the hallway and up the steps. He felt foolish doing it (how could a *cat* harm him?) but he did it just the same.

He saw nothing in the hall or on the stairs. In his bedroom he closed the door before he turned on the light and then, using the flashlight to help him, he searched the room thoroughly. This time he looked under the bed.

Wherever the cat was, it wasn't in this room. And, harmless and ordinary though it might be, it wasn't going to get in while he was sleeping. Luckily it was not a warm night and he would do without ventilation for once by sleeping with both the door and the window closed. Not, in the case of the window, because the cat could get through it from wherever it now was; but the cat must have got into the house that way in the first place, and what *else* might decide to come that way?

For some strange reason he wished he'd brought one of his guns upstairs with him.

But eventually he slept, and slept soundly.

CHAPTER FIFTEEN

The mind thing had panicked when he had heard the man he now knew was Doc Staunton call out: 'All right, Cat . . .'

It was the reaction, mostly, from learning that, in addition to being the optimum host he could possibly expect to find, the man suspected something close to the truth, and could be dangerous. He'd had only contempt for any human intellect he'd hitherto encountered.

But Staunton was the perfect host – a top electronicist, solvent and free to travel, single and without responsibilities. He'd listened with increasing fascination to the conversation between Staunton and Miss Talley, and to what Staunton had dictated to her.

And, although this was extrapolating, he felt sure that Staunton would have, or have access to, every item of equipment that he would need. With Staunton as a host, he could be back on his own planet as soon as within a few weeks – and a hero of his race for having discovered a planet definitely worthy of colonisation.

But why had he made the initial mistake of drawing back and hiding when Miss Talley had looked up suddenly and had caught a glimpse of him in the hall? If only he'd remembered – which he hadn't because of his excitement over the things he was learning about Staunton – to act like an ordinary cat! Once glimpsed, he should have strolled on out in the kitchen, right into their sight. If he'd acted friendly they might have petted him, if they were people who liked cats;

possibly given him a bowl of milk and then let him out when he miaouwed and scratched at the door. At worst, if they were people who didn't like cats, they'd have opened the door and shooed him out with a broom. And he'd have been free, those many hours ago, to make an inconspicuous death and be back in his own body, his shell, under the back steps of the Gross farmhouse.

Free to plan and then choose his next host, one who could move his shell from the Gross farm to the Staunton place here, near enough for Staunton's bed to be within his range of perception so he could take over Staunton's mind the first time Staunton slept.

That is what he should have done, certainly. But having once hidden, he'd decided that the safest thing to do was to stay hidden until, through the first door or window left open, he could escape and be free. But Staunton – damn him for being so clever! – had left nothing open. And now, because of the catprints in that scattered flour, Staunton knew for sure that he was here.

How much more did Staunton guess? He'd definitely suspected something, even before he'd left the house, to have set that tell tale trap with the flour. Alone in the house and wandering around to explore, he'd not known that he was walking in the thin film of flour until the sensitive pads of his feet had told him he was walking in something, and he'd looked down, too late. How hard he'd tried to think of a way of obliterating those paw prints, or of cleaning up the flour and spreading fresh flour! It was simply impossible, in this tiny body he now occupied. Not the cleaning up of the flour; he could have licked it up, but the problem of spreading fresh flour and doing it evenly and neatly was insuperable. He might have been able to open the cupboard door to get at the flour sifter but, small as he was and without hands, there was no way at all of his using it as the man had done. No way at all.

His real panic had come when Staunton, returning, had called him, addressing him as one intelligent being speaking to another. Had Staunton determined by logic or by intuition that a cat trapped in his house wasn't really a cat at all? It seemed incredible that he had worked it out from such slender evidence.

But it could be. Staunton, he must remember, was a scientist. The mind thing's contact, from inside, with human minds had been with the mind of a boy not yet out of high school, and the mind of a stupid and barely literate old man. Perhaps there were things, many things, in this world that neither Tommy nor Gross knew or even suspected, but that would be elementary to Staunton. Perhaps there were species here on Earth which *were* capable of taking over and using hosts, as his species did. Perhaps some human beings could, with special abilities or special training, take over lesser creatures. Well, he'd find the answer to that in Staunton's mind if and when he could take it over.

The immediate problem was escape, getting out of this house. Suicide was definitely out, even if he could find the means of accomplishing it here. It had been the unexplained series of suicides of men, animals, and birds that had roused Staunton's scientific curiosity in the first place. Having one happen right here in his own house, and under these circumstances, might be just the final evidence that would convince him completely of what he now – the mind thing hoped – only suspected.

There was, he realised now, only one thing he could possibly do, and that was to come out of hiding in the morning, let Staunton see him, and try to the utmost of his ability to act like a cat, an ordinary cat. It would be dangerous, but there was no alternative. The danger was not that for any reason Staunton might kill him; that would free him immediately – and if Staunton knew about hosts, killing him was the last thing he'd do. He'd know that killing the host would free the being controlling it. The danger was that Staunton, knowing this, would catch him and keep him caged for study. If nothing worse, that would waste time; maybe he wouldn't be able to escape until the cat died a natural death, and cats lived for years. The danger was even greater that Staunton would know the psychological tests that could distinguish a controlled creature from a free one.

And if Staunton could prove that—? There'd been some vague knowledge in Tommy Hoffman's mind that something called truth serum existed. If Staunton injected that and forced him to communicate under its influence, he was through. He'd be forced to communicate the location of his own body, helpless at the Gross farm, and they'd have him.

Even, he realised in sudden despair, Staunton's caging the cat for study and keeping it caged indefinitely, would cause his death if the cat lived long enough. In less than the natural length of a cat's life his own body would perish for lack of nourishment. The immersion in nutrient solution he'd had Gross give it was enough to last for months, but not for as much as a year. Being imprisoned indefinitely in the body of any host unable to feed him would be fatal for his own body.

He spent the whole night thinking, weighing odds. He considered leaping against a window in the hope that the glass would break and let him through – but the objection to that was the same as that to an attempt at suicide. Even if successful, either would confirm his captor's suspicions.

He could only hope that they *were* only suspicions and not certainties, and that Staunton would let him go in the morning. He could only hope so, and do his best to make the man think that he was only an ordinary cat, after all.

Doc Staunton hadn't got to bed until one o'clock, and hadn't gone to sleep until a good hour after that, so he slept later than he usually did, even on vacation. A little after ten in the morning he woke from a confused dream in which he was trying to design a metering device for a satellite but couldn't remember, or find out from anyone, just what it was supposed to meter. He lay a moment trying to recapture the earlier part of the dream, which still evaded him, and then suddenly remembered the matter of the cat in this house; he forgot about the dream and lay thinking about the cat.

But the matter didn't seem nearly so sinister now, in the light of day, as it had last night. Hadn't he been exaggerating the possibility of any connection between having a stray cat in his house and the strange deaths that had happened during the previous ten days?

Well ... probably. But still there was something that needed explanation. It wasn't strange that a cat might enter a house out of curiosity, or out of hunger, through a door or window that had been left open. He doubted that many cats did, at least ones that had homes; but it was not too odd that one should do so. The strange thing was its method of entry.

Yet even that could be explained – if the cat was a homeless one, and hungry. Perhaps it had climbed the tree because it had seen a bird sleeping there and thought it might catch the bird. And then, once out on that particular branch and losing its quarry, the sight of an open window just might tempt it. Any cat, even a stray one, would know that there was food in houses.

But then it had hidden in the hall, near the kitchen doorway almost as though spying on them, listening to their conversation. And hiding ever since ...

Still, if it was a cat that had never had a home and, possibly because boys or a farmer had once thrown stones at it, was afraid of human beings ...

He got out of bed and started dressing, deciding that he'd find the cat first, no matter how much searching he'd have to do, and then make up his mind.

He remembered there was a pair of fairly heavy leather gloves in a drawer of the dresser; he got them and put them in a pocket. If he was forced to corner the cat and catch it, and if it was a cat that was wild and might fight against being picked up – and even domestic cats sometimes did that with strangers – those gloves would come in handy. With them on, he should be able to handle it. From the size of the paw prints it had left in the flour, it certainly wasn't very large. And wild though it might be, it definitely wasn't a wildcat; his brief study of the prints had convinced him of that. He'd seen prints of a wildcat and they were quite different.

When he left the room he'd slept in he closed the door behind him. Might as well be systematic about his hunting, take the upstairs rooms before he went downstairs, and close the door of each after he'd searched it. He took the bathroom first, since he had to go there anyway, and then the other two bedrooms.

The cat wasn't upstairs.

He saw it when he was halfway down the steps. It was sitting calmly at the front door, as a cat or dog does when it wants to be let out.

It didn't look dangerous in the slightest. It was a small grey cat, perfectly ordinary-looking. It didn't look at all starved and it didn't seem frightened of him. In fact, it looked up at him as though quite friendly. It miaouwed and scratched lightly against the door.

Just a cat, a very normal cat, asking to be let out of the house.

Almost too normal, Doc thought, for a cat that had hidden from him for so long yesterday. He sat down on the bottom step of the staircase and stared at it, still at the front door, still wanting out. 'Miaouw,' it said.

Doc shook his head. 'Not just yet, Cat. I'll let you out later, I guess, but I want to have a little talk with you first. And how about breakfast? I'm going to have some myself.'

He got up and went into the kitchen, not looking behind him until he was at the refrigerator.

The cat had followed him, but not closely at his heels. Now it was sitting staring at him. Then, as though it had a sudden idea, it went past him – but, he noticed, circling far enough to keep out of his reach – and to the kitchen door. It scratched at that, miaouwed again, and looked back at him. It was saying 'Let me out, please' as clearly as a cat can say it. An ordinary cat that is.

Doc shook his head firmly. 'No, Cat. Later, but not now. I want to think it over first.'

He got milk from the refrigerator and put a bowl of it down on the floor. The cat didn't approach it; it stayed at the door while he got his own breakfast, frying himself a couple of eggs and boiling water for instant coffee.

When he took his breakfast across the room and sat down at the big table with it, the cat left the door and went to the bowl of milk. It started lapping hungrily.

'Nice kitty,' Doc said through a bite of egg. 'How'd you like to stay around and visit me a while?'

The cat didn't answer, but, staring at it, Doc decided he hadn't really been kidding. It would be pleasant to have a cat around, something to talk to. And if there was really anything strange about the cat, it would give him a chance to watch it for a while.

Of course he couldn't keep it shut up indefinitely, not without suffocating himself on hot days. Or could he, by buying some half-screens, the kind you could fit into a window opened halfway? There seemed to be so few flies around that the owner of the house had never bothered to screen it. Yes, Doc thought, he could go even further than that and have a carpenter come out from town and fit him a full set of screens. He'd been wanting to add some small improvement to the house as a token of gratitude for being allowed to use it. And after all there were *some* flies, and moths at night unless you closed the window when you put on the lights. A set of screens would be just about right as a contribution. Maybe he'd have them put on, cat or no cat.

Of course he didn't want to steal anyone's cat if its owner really wanted it back. He could take care of that by asking around town. If he found an owner, the man would probably gladly sell it to him for a few dollars, unless it was a child's particular pet. Cats are plentiful and cheap around a farming community, and they breed so fast that the supply always exceeds the demand.

When he left to go back to MIT to resume his teaching, he'd have to find a home for it before leaving, but that shouldn't be too difficult if he was willing to subsidise the deal by offering a light bonus along with the cat. Feeding one more cat wouldn't matter much to a farmer who already had several, and even the most domesticated cats largely earn their own living in this kind of country by keeping down the field mice.

'Cat,' he said, 'speaking seriously, how *would* you like to live here a while? Oh, and by the way what's your name?' The cat, still lapping, milk, didn't answer.

'All right, you won't tell me,' Doc said. 'In that case you're all set with a brand new name, the one I've been calling you. *Cat*. It's appropriate . . . I hope.'

The cat had drunk only about half of the milk, but that was all right; he'd probably given it much too much for a cat its size to drink, and it was back sitting at the door again.

'Miaouw,' it said.

'I understand, Cat,' Doc said. 'A call of nature, and that's not surprising considering how long you've been here. But the very fact that you want out so badly proves that you're housebroken. I'll take care of things.'

He'd finished eating by then and went across to the door that led to the basement stairs, went down them. Someone who had stayed here, luckily, had done a lot of sawing for something or other; there was a fairish pile of dry sawdust in one corner of the basement. He found a shallow carton of about the proper dimensions and filled it with sawdust, took it up to the kitchen and put it in a corner.

'You'll have to use that, Cat,' he said. 'I'm afraid you're not going out for a few days.'

The cat looked at the box of sawdust but stayed at the door. 'Miaouw,' it said. Very plaintively.

'You're an outdoor cat, maybe, and never used a sawdust box?' Doc asked it. 'Well, you'll learn, when the pressure gets high enough.'

He took his breakfast dishes to the sink and started washing them.

'Tell you what, Cat,' he said over his shoulder. 'Let's give it a try together, for a few days. For that length of time, I'll clear up if you don't figure out how to use the sawdust.

'And if you turn out to like me and I turn out to like you, then I'll give you your choice – you can go out, and come back if you wish or never darken my doorway again. Fair enough?'

The cat didn't answer except possibly by not answering: it stayed by the door.

Doc decided to go about the things he had to do and pay no more attention to it for a while, to see what it did.

The mind thing, helpless in the cat-body of which it could not rid itself without giving away more than it already had, stayed by the door. The bladder- and bowel-pressure were considerable by now. And Staunton obviously wasn't going to let him out of the house. He didn't feel, except in the objective sense of being aware of, the pain of the body he was in; but that was not the problem. Staunton expected to keep him shut up for several days. He had to let this body evacuate itself before then or the very fact that it had not would be an additional cause for suspicion. Staunton had more than enough already. The question then was whether to use the floor or the box. If he pretended to be strictly an outdoor cat, unused to using a sawdust box, and dirtied the floor now and as often as he could, would that disgust Staunton and cause his release earlier than if he pretended to be housebroken to the extent of using the box?

He watched Staunton emotionlessly – not hating him, because the emotion of hatred was as alien to him as the feeling of mercy – except, in both cases, towards his own kind.

Suddenly a thought came to him. Staunton, with his suspicions already aroused, might well make an attempt to find out where the cat he was using had come from, who had owned it, how and when it had disappeared. And other facts about it – including the degree of its being housebroken. Any discrepancy would make Staunton still more suspicious. The mind thing knew he should examine the mind of his current host and let his actions as a cat correspond with what that particular cat would do under given circumstances, and guide his actions accordingly.

It took him only a second to locate that particular memory in the cat's brain. He walked over to the sawdust box.

Staunton, at the sink, glanced down casually. 'Attaboy,' he said. 'Nice kitty.'

Yes, the mind thing knew that this was what he should have done all along, examined the mind of his particular host and acted as the host would have acted under the same circumstances, any time he was under observation. Had he only done that yesterday when the woman had first seen him in the hallway – walked out into the kitchen and looked at the two of them calmly, instead of hiding . . .

This chore taken care of, he thought what he should do next to play his part to the hilt. He'd lie down and sleep a while, probably. Find a soft comfortable place to rest in. There was a sofa in the living-room. He padded through the doorway, jumped up on to the sofa, and curled himself up comfortably.

Staunton was standing there in the doorway. 'Okay, Cat,' he said. 'Might as well make yourself at home. What made you hide yesterday and last night?' Then he went back into the kitchen.

The mind thing let his cat-body rest and sleep, but his own mind was thinking what a fool he'd been letting himself panic, and hiding twice, once when the woman had seen him in the hallway, once when, after he'd walked through the flour, Staunton had come home after midnight.

He let himself explore his host's mind thoroughly now, at leisure. Losing a few days being shut up here would be an annoyance but still only a minor delay. Apparently Staunton wasn't going to try him out with specific psychological tests, but just keep him under general observation. It should be easy for the mind thing, now that he knew what he had to do.

It was beginning to get a little warm and Staunton was going around opening all of the downstairs windows – but each only a carefully calculated scant two inches, just enough so a medium-small cat couldn't get through.

A little later, Staunton was looking down at him. 'Cat,' he said, 'I'm going downtown a while; you hold the fort. I'll pick up some cat food or liver or something. While you're here, I might as well be the perfect host.'

The mind thing almost made his present host jump; then he realised Staunton was using the word 'host' in a different sense. He blinked at him sleepily.

When Staunton walked to the front door he jumped off the sofa and ran after him, to stay in character. But Staunton reached down a hand and took him gently by the scruff of the neck – the first time there had been physical contact between them – and held him back until he was able to get the door closed from the outside, with the cat inside.

In Bartlesville Doc made his first stop at the office of the *Clarion.*

Hollis looked up from the typewriter he'd been hammering. 'Hi,' he said. 'What's new?'

'Nothing startling, Ed. Just wanted to ask you a question. Know anybody looking for a missing cat?'

Hollis laughed. 'A cat? Cats are a dime a dozen around here. If one wanders off, it wanders off. Why? You find one?'

'Yes. And thought I might keep it a while if it wants to stay with me. But I wouldn't if I knew whoever owned it really wanted it. It might be a child's pet, for instance.'

'There's that. Well, I can run an ad in the lost and found column for you. Deadline for that is Friday noon; that's when we start closing the forms.'

Staunton thought a moment. He might as well save stopping in again by giving Hollis the ad now. He said, 'Okay, I'll give you the ad now. "Found, small grey cat." And give it a box number; I'll check with you next week to see if there's been an answer.'

'Sure.' Hollis jotted it down on a pad. 'But hey, I know whose cat it might be. I was out at Kramer's last week and he had a small grey cat, among several others. That's out your way, so it might be his.'

'Just where out my way?'

'Next door to the Gross farm. You know where that is; heard you were out there with the sheriff after the suicide. It's the farm east of theirs; Loursat has the one to the west.'

'Thanks, Ed. I'll drop in on my way home to find out. You run that ad, though, unless I tell you not to. So long.'

When he did his shopping, Doc bought two cans of cat food. One can was surely enough for a cat that size for two days so two cans would run him until he let the cat out to see if it would stay around and come back, or would run away.

From the drugstore he phoned Miss Talley to ask her whether she was still sure she'd be done by Thursday noon, and whether she'd learned anything new. Yes, she was sure she'd be finished by the time she'd predicted, and no, she'd learned nothing interesting; she wouldn't have much chance to put or keep her ear to the ground until she'd finished the typing.

And, she wanted to know, had he found a cat at his house? He told her about the cat and about his decision in connection with it.

On his way home he stopped at the farm east of the Gross farm. There were two cats on the front porch. Both were about the same size as the grey one and could easily be from the same litter.

A plump, friendly woman answered his knock on the door.

'I'm Ralph Staunton,' he told her. 'I live in the last house down the road. I—'

'Oh, yes,' she said. 'I've heard your name, and I've seen you drive past. Won't you step in?' She moved back to make way for him.

'I might as well, but just for a moment. It's nothing very important, Mrs Kramer. I hear you have a grey cat. I've found one, about the size of those two cats on the porch and I wondered—'

'Oh, yes. I hadn't seen him for a day or two and wondered if anything had happened to him.'

'Nothing has, except that he wandered into my house. Thought I might like to keep him. Would you consider selling him?'

She laughed. 'Sell him? Oh, goodness no. But you can have him if you want him. We've got three other cats – our old cat had a litter of six last time and we were able to find homes for only three of them. And she's going to have another litter soon.' She shook her head. 'I'm afraid after that we're going to get rid of her or take her to the vet and have her spayed. Else we'll be drowning in cats.'

'Thanks a lot,' Doc said. 'I'll be glad to take him, and I'll promise to find a home for him when I leave at the end of the summer – or take him back with me if I can't. That is, if he stays with me.'

'But I thought you said—'

'I've got him shut in the house right now, to see if he'll get used to it and to me and want to stay. But I can't do that forever so in a few more days I'll have to let him out – and we'll have to see whether he'll want to stay with me or come back to you. I can't very well keep him against his will; cats are very independent people.'

'Oh dear. I guess you're right, but I do hope he'll stay with you. His name is Jerry, by the way.'

'Not any more, if he stays with me,' Doc said. 'I've given him a new name. I call him Cat.'

Mrs Kramer laughed.

The cat must have heard Doc Staunton coming because it was waiting inside the door and tried to get past him, but he managed to catch it. 'No, Cat,' he said, this time taking it up in his arms and kicking the door shut with his foot. 'I explained that to you; you're in stir for a few days. Then you can make up your mind whether you want to keep on being Cat with me, or go back to being Jerry with the Kramers. I know who you are now, you see.'

He put it down on the sofa and stood looking down at it. 'Or do I?' he added softly.

It wasn't until he went to open a window wider and remembered in time not to, that it occurred to him that he'd forgotten to check on getting screens fitted while he was in town. Well, he'd be in town again tomorrow; one day wouldn't matter.

CHAPTER SIXTEEN

One day didn't make the slightest difference, it turned out, on his ordering the screens. He went into town again the next day, Thursday, and saw Hank Purdy, the town's only really good rough carpenter. He learned that Hank had more work than he could handle for at least a week. He promised to come out later the following week, take measurements and make an estimate. Doc might have found someone else who could do the job sooner, but he liked Hank, whom he knew from the poker games in the back room at the tavern, and decided he'd rather wait and have Hank do the job. After all, he wasn't going to keep the cat shut up more than another few days, and after that the house would be in no more immediate need of screens than it had been all along. Besides, the weather was mild and having the windows as they were now, each of them raised about two inches, provided plenty of ventilation.

He parked the station wagon in front of Miss Talley's little house. She must have seen him stopping there, because she had the door opened before he reached it.

'Come in, Doctor. All ready for you. Sit down, and I'll bring the manuscripts. And my notebook.'

'Thanks, Miss Talley, but I don't think I'm going to dictate those two letters today. I've decided I want a few days to think things over before I send them. And I may as well wait to write until I'm ready to mail them; something else might happen and I can put any subsequent information in the letter.'

'All right, if you think so.' She picked up a large brown envelope and gave it to him. 'Want to read this now anyway?'

He shook his head. 'Might as well read it at home. I'd rather talk a few minutes, if you've time.'

She had time, she told him. He told her about the cat. 'I started out being scared of it, or about its being there.' He laughed. 'You and your talk about possession did that to me, I suppose. But now I feel just the opposite. I hope it sticks around; it keeps me from getting lonesome, I think it's a perfectly normal cat, Miss Talley.'

'And Buck was a perfectly normal dog, until he ran under your car. In spite of what you say, Doctor, I'm a little worried about its living there with you. I suppose it's silly of me, but – I do worry.'

'I'll be all right, Miss Talley. I'm afraid I'm beginning to think we both went a bit overboard on this.'

'Possibly, Doctor ... Will you promise me you'll send those letters, and the reports, to the two friends you mentioned?'

Doc sighed. 'All right, I'll send them. Just want a couple of days to think it over first.'

'All right. For the rest of this week I'll be staying home, that is, early afternoons; so any day you want to come and dictate them ...'

That evening after he had finished washing the dishes he went into the living-room and sat on the sofa; the cat was already there and he reached over and stroked its sleek fur. The cat purred.

'Well, Cat, getting to like it here? And to like me? Let's see; this is Thursday evening. Let's set a date for giving you your choice, a date and an hour. How does Monday strike you? Let's see; I've been feeding you about the middle of the afternoon. I'll let you go out – if you still want to go out – about the middle of the morning. That'll give you time to think it over before you get hungry again.

'If I go into town I won't stay long; I'll go when I let you out, and be back by noon. Waiting and ready to feed you if you come back. Fair enough?'

The cat didn't answer, but it still purred.

Doc said, 'If it relieves a worry on your part, the Kramers gave you to me; they don't want you back. Oh, they'll take you if you want to go home to them. They'll feed you, and forgive you.

'Yes, I know who you are, and that your name was Jerry there. Might have kept that name if another male cat had come with you. I'd have called him Tom. Tom and Jerry. Ever tasted one? They're good. But that's irrelevant. Which are you going to prefer, the Kramers or me?'

He got up and took a comfortable chair facing the sofa. He stared at the cat from across the room.

'Cat, why *did* you hide? Why did you come in an upstairs window? Don't you know cats just don't do that? Damn it, why didn't you act all along as you're acting now?'

The cat stretched languorously and then curled up again and closed its eyes.

'Cat.' Doc said it sharply and the cat opened its eyes again and stared at him.

'Cat, don't go to sleep on me. I'm talking to you, and sleeping isn't polite when you're being spoken to. Cat, you used to live on the farm next to the Grosses. Did you know *their* cat? The one that committed suicide the night Gross did? Don't tell me it wasn't suicide, that cat jumping right into the jaws of a vicious dog it must have known was there. If it was suicide, why? And if it wasn't, what was it?'

The cat's eyes had closed, but somehow Doc felt that it wasn't asleep.

'And an owl killed itself that same night. What do you know about that? And before that, along with Tommy Hoffman's death we had a field mouse that got itself killed, seemingly deliberately. And a dog. Do you know that I was the one who ran over the dog? And that it had been hiding beside the road until my car got just the right distance away – only a few yards – and then ran right under my wheels? I'll *swear* that one was deliberate – especially since they tell me that dog was car-shy.

'Two human beings, four animals – that we know of. Of course any other human suicides we'd know about, but how many more animals, especially ones out in the woods and not under observation, might have brought about their own deaths recently after— After what? After they'd served the purpose of whoever, or *whatever*, was using them?'

Outside, crickets were chirping, thousands of crickets. Doc's mind wandered and he thought how strange it was that one could tell the temperature, almost exactly, by timing the interval between the chirps of a cricket. A cricket was a thermometer. There were many strange things in nature. Lemmings, with their periodical suicidal migrations to and into the sea. Group insanity? Or do the lemmings know somcthing that we don't know?

He heard the crickets, watched the black night press against the window pane. He turned back to the cat.

'Cat,' he said, 'why did those other animals kill themselves? If you're like them, why don't you? Is the only reason you're alive the fact that there isn't any way of killing yourself shut up here? Wait a minute, I'll find out.'

He left the living-room and went across the hall and into the third downstairs room, a small room that was only partly furnished and used mostly for storage. Except for items that were already there, Doc used it only to store his fishing tackle and boots, his guns and ammunition. Although he knew there was open season on nothing worth hunting in

Wisconsin in summer, he'd brought a pistol and a rifle for target practice and a shotgun mostly because it was a brand-new one and he wanted a chance to try it out. All these things he'd had shipped ahead of him before his flight to Green Bay; he'd picked them up there after he'd bought the used station wagon which he'd sell before flying back at the end of the summer.

He took the pistol, a .38-calibre S & W Special and took a cardboard rifle target from a package of them. In the doorway between the hall and the living-room he put the square of cardboard down on the floor and went back to the chair he'd been sitting in. He cocked the gun and saw the cat raise its head at the sudden click.

'Listen, Cat,' he said, 'let's try this for size. If you're only wanting out of here so you can find a way to kill yourself, I'll save you the trouble. If you understand what I'm saying and want me to shoot you, prove it by going to the doorway there. Sit down on the target, that's all you have to do.'

For a moment the cat blinked at him sleepily and then it put its head down again and went back to sleep – or pretended to. If it understood his offer, it wasn't having any.

Doc sighed; he hadn't really expected the cat to go and sit on the target. If it was – well, if it *wasn't* altogether a cat, it would be giving itself away by doing that. And shooting it would have been the last thing he'd have done under those circumstances. Especially with a gun he hadn't bothered to load.

He put the pistol and the target back where he'd taken them from and went into the kitchen. He'd have a final can of beer and a snack, if something in the refrigerator looked good to him, and then go to bed.

The sound of the refrigerator door brought the cat from the sofa into the kitchen. It paid no attention to anything he said but it had come to recognise that sound – or more likely was familiar with it from having been in the Kramers' kitchen – and he couldn't get anything from the refrigerator without the cat being there watching him. It didn't beg, but it was on the spot and ready for any handouts he might give it.

He found a few slices of liverwurst, dropped one into the cat's dish, and made himself a sandwich with the rest of it. He opened a can of beer and went over to the table. The cat finished its share of the liverwurst and went back to the living-room, presumably to lie on the sofa again. Doc had managed to convince it that once he'd taken his own food to the table, further begging was useless. Besides, the cat couldn't be really hungry. It came to him when he went to the refrigerator only because it wanted a snack of something different from its staple diet of cat food and milk.

Doc got the flashlight before he turned off the lights; he still used one to light himself up to the bedroom as he had the first night the cat had been in the house, but not for quite the same reason. Now he simply didn't want to step on or fall over the cat in darkness. Since it could see in the dark itself, it couldn't realise that he couldn't.

The next day, Friday, nothing special happened. He made his usual trip into town but found no mail waiting for him, and didn't have to do any shopping. He dropped in at the newspaper office on the excuse of cancelling his ad about having found a cat, but mostly just to talk to Ed Hollis a while to make sure nothing unusual had happened since the day before. Nothing had, except that the Garners had found a buyer for their farm and were planning to move west, possibly to the Ozarks, possibly on to California. And Gus Hoffman, Tommy's father, was putting an ad in the Bartlesville paper offering his farm for sale, and was planning to run one in the Green Bay papers too.

'My guess,' Hollis said, 'is that that means Charlotte's pregnant. The Garners moving, I mean.'

'You'd better not put a guess like that in your paper, Ed.'

Hollis looked at Doc so resentfully that Doc apologised.

'But why,' Hollis wondered aloud, 'would that make Gus Hoffman decide to move too? I mean, with Tommy dead, a scandal – not that there'd be much of one anyway – wouldn't hurt Gus.'

'You're a damn fool, Ed. Hoffman will stick close to the Garners from here on in. He hasn't a wife or a child – but he's got a grandson or granddaughter on the way. Illegitimate or not, he'll be crazy about that kid.'

'Hell, yes. Why didn't I think of that? Probably, wherever they go, he'll talk the Garners into letting him come in with them on a farm big enough for him too. And Charlotte will be a very young widow named Mrs Hoffman and Gus will be her father-in-law. So the kid will even have Gus's name, and Gus will again have something to live for.'

Doc had so few errands to do in town that day that he got back quite early and decided he might as well spend the rest of the afternoon fishing. It would be his first time fishing since he'd run over the dog and had through that episode become interested in the strange details surrounding the death of Tommy Hoffman.

He was glad to notice that the cat had apparently reconciled itself to staying in his house; at least – although he took precautions both times – it made no effort to get past him when he let himself in to get his fishing equipment or let himself out after he had gathered what he needed. It was becoming acclimated.

Or was it because it understood everything he'd told it and knew that he'd promised it its freedom on Monday anyway? He put that thought out of his mind and decided to concentrate on the pleasure of his hike to the nearest trout stream and his fishing when he reached it.

The fishing was quite good, considering that it was the wrong time of day for it. Within an hour he had five medium-sized trout in his creel. Enjoyable as the fishing was in itself, that satisfied him. It was more than he could eat today, possibly even tomorrow, even with the help of a cat. And fresh trout were infinitely more tasty than ones that had been in the refrigerator for more than a day or so.

After his return he cleaned the fish and cooked three of them. He ate two and the cat had no trouble disposing of the third, so avidly that Doc was amused. He said, 'All right, Cat, consider that a bribe if you want. But over all, if you decide to say with me, I'll promise you a trout about every third day. Not every day, though.'

At breakfast Monday morning he gave thought to his decision to release the cat about mid-morning, then see whether, after five or six hours of freedom, it would return at the usual feeding time he had established for it. Oh, he'd do it; he couldn't keep, didn't want to keep a cat shut up any longer than the few days he'd decided to keep it. He'd let it out; it would be a free agent as to whether it returned to him or not. But there was one little thing he could do and might as well do. He had a pair of excellent binoculars with him. The moment he let the cat out of the door he'd take them upstairs. From the window of one or another of the rooms up there he'd be able to follow it quite a distance, no matter which direction it went. If it headed towards the Kramer farm, he'd probably never see it again; if it went any other direction he might. If it stayed around the immediate vicinity, just wandering in the yard, it would be almost certain to come back in if he called it at feeding time.

Looking out, he saw that a light drizzle had started and wondered if a real rain was coming. If so, the cat probably wouldn't go out at all; cats hate water. But the drizzle lasted only ten or fifteen minutes, just enough to lay the dust and moisten the ground a bit.

At ten o'clock exactly – might as well keep his promise on the dot, he thought; he'd said the middle of the morning –

he went into the living-room past the cat on the sofa and to the front door. He opened it wide and said, 'Well, Cat, want out a while?'

The cat understood the action if not the words. It got down from the sofa, stretched itself leisurely and unhurriedly, and then padded past him through the open doorway.

Quickly he got the binoculars and went upstairs with them. He tried the window of the front bedroom first and it turned out to be the right one; the cat was about halfway across the front yard, heading for the place where the road dead-ended. It was neither hurrying nor dawdling, walking unconcernedly at the pace of a cat that knows where it's going but is in no hurry to get there.

Probably heading back to the Kramers', he thought. Well, if that's what it wanted that was all right, and maybe all to the good. The Kramer woman's attitude in giving it to him had shown him that it might not be as easy as he had assumed for him to find a home for it later. And, since he certainly wouldn't abandon an animal, he might have to take it back to Boston with him, and that would be a confounded nuisance.

But when it reached the dead end of the road, the cat stopped. It turned its head and stared back at the house it had just left. Doc stepped hastily back from the window, but kept the cat in the field of the binoculars. Was it looking back in indecision as to whether it wanted to go home, after all? Or was it watching to see if *he* was watching it? He didn't think it had seen him, or that it could see him now that he'd stepped back from the window.

It stayed there half a minute, either making up its mind or making sure that it wasn't being watched. Which?

Then it started again, going a little faster this time, and not down the road that would take it to the Kramers'. It went right across the end of the road instead, into the woods. He could follow it only a few yards after that.

Doc put down the binoculars and scratched his head. After all, its behaviour was probably perfectly normal, but—

Then he remembered the drizzle that had fallen a while half an hour ago. Because of that, it would be leaving paw prints. And why shouldn't he follow them a while, for as far as he could, and see if he could find out where it was going? After all, he had nothing else to do right now that had to be done today, and a walk would be as pleasant a way of filling in the time as any other.

He started at once, delaying only to put on a hat and to hang a raincoat over his arm, in case the rain might start again. The cat's pawprints were clear across the yard and once he bent down and studied a few prints to memorise their size and shape; he didn't want to end up tracking some other small animal instead.

It was harder going when he got to the woods, for the prints didn't show in grassy areas, nor did they show at all clearly under trees; the rain hadn't been hard enough to work its way through the leaves and under every tree was a completely dry circle.

Then it got easier again when he realised that the cat, wherever it was going, had been travelling in an almost perfect straight line.

After that, Doc was able to make better time; he simply walked in a straight line himself across any grassy or dry areas and didn't have to cast about on the other side to pick up the trail; it would be right at the place he himself came out.

He was at least a mile and a half into the woods when the trail ended. Suddenly, at the edge of a small stream of water that wasn't over four feet wide at this point. Had the cat jumped across it? He jumped across it himself and tried to pick up the trail on the other side. It simply wasn't there. The ground for several feet on either side of the stream was bare and moist; the cat's prints leading down *to* the water were as clear as any he'd found. But the cat hadn't jumped across or its prints would be just as clear as the ones leading to the stream.

Not quite daring to allow himself to think as yet, Doc followed the stream along the far side. Downstream, of course. The current was slow.

It took him only about twenty paces to see what he had been afraid he would see, ever since he reached the stream.

In the water, drowned, one small grey cat.

It was even more obviously a suicide than the dog that had run in front of his car, thc owl that had flown through a window, the field mouse that had attacked Tommy Hoffman, or the other cat that had attacked a vicious dog ten times its size.

And it had lived with him for days. It had refused his gambit with the pistol, it had not tried to starve itself or to bring about its own death in any other way.

It had waited till it could commit the act unobserved, so deep in the woods that – if he had not still had a residue of suspicion and the advantage of that brief drizzle that had made it trackable – it's body would probably never have been found.

Had it, after all, understood every word he'd said to it and intelligently decided, when he promised to let it go this morning, that it would stand less chance of giving itself away by waiting that long than by making any attempt to die sooner?

But – suicide is no end in itself. What was the purpose?

The cat *had been* an ordinary cat once; he'd traced its origin. The dog *had been* an ordinary dog until it had run away from its master only a short time before it had found death under the wheels of a car.

Was *something* using animals, each for some mysterious purpose, and then getting free of them by causing them to kill themselves?

What had been in the mind of that cat, all the time it had been with him?

And what of the human beings, Tommy Hoffman and Siegfried Gross? Had something been using them, controlling their minds, causing them to commit some action too difficult for an animal host, and then causing them to kill themselves?

But what? And why?

He remembered stroking the cat and enjoying its purring under his hand. What had he really been stroking?

He shuddered. The slight scare he'd had the night the cat had hidden from him – had that been only Tuesday night? – was nothing now. It had been based on nothing more than hunch or intuition.

Then he'd been only guessing. Now he *knew.*

But *what* did he know? Only that he was frightened.

He found a stick and manoeuvred the small body to the edge of the water where he could reach it. He picked it up gingerly and carried it back with him to the house. He wrapped it in an old blanket and put it in the back of the station wagon. To take it to the laboratory in Green Bay and have it autopsied? He hadn't decided yet, but the body was there now if he should decide to take it in. But what could he tell them to check for? There was certainly no remote suspicion of rabies this time; the cat had been – or seemed – completely normal when he had let it out less than an hour before.

He smoked a pipe and thought a while and then realized what was the first thing he must do. He got the envelope with the copies of the statement he had dictated to Miss Talley and drove to town with them. He should have mailed them sooner; now he'd get them in the mail as soon as he could add the story of the cat to what they already contained and dictate the covering letters.

Miss Talley was not at home. There was a note on her door, 'Back about 3 p.m.' It was time for lunch anyway, so he drove back to the downtown district and ate, then killed time at the tavern drinking a few beers. He had several chances to get into conversation, but he didn't feel like talking. He could hardly bring up suddenly now what he was thinking about; there was too much to tell all at once to anyone with whom he hadn't talked before. And that left only Miss Talley.

He watched the clock and reached her place a few minutes early, but she was there.

'Doctor!' she said, when she saw his face. 'Come in. Has something new happened?'

He nodded a little grimly. 'It's about the cat. But I want to dictate it as an addendum to the statement I dictated to you last week. If you'll get your notebook—'

Miss Talley got it, and her eyes danced as excitedly as her pencil point as he talked and she wrote. He told the whole story of the cat, from her first glimpse of it during his previous dictation to his finding it drowned in the little creek. He went into detail and it took him over an hour.

Miss Talley looked up then. 'Doctor! Besides mailing these to your two friends, you've *got* to go to the sheriff now. Or call in the FBI – or *something*, if he won't take it seriously.'

Doc nodded slowly. 'I'm going to, Miss Talley. I'll tell you my plans before I leave, but first, while I'm dictating, let me give you the two covering letters that go with the statements that I'm going to mail out.'

He dictated again, and the letters ran longer than he had anticipated; it was almost five o'clock when he had finished. 'Miss Talley, about how long do you think it will take you to transcribe all that?'

'A few hours, possibly four, but I'll start it right away; I won't even eat until I've finished. While I'm doing it you can go see the sheriff and—'

'No, I want to wait till I have a copy of the full statement to have him read when I see him. It'll impress him more that way, I think. After all, outside of the grey cat episode, nothing in here will be new to him, and for me just to tell him over again – well, I'd rather have him read the statement.

'And I'm not going to let you work all evening without eating, or waste time cooking for yourself either. Put your coat on and we'll eat together in town. Then I'll drive you back here and leave you. You can do your typing, and in the morning I'll talk to the sheriff and get those letters in the mail – airmail special delivery. It'll be too late by the time you finish this evening, even if I'd let you work straight through.'

'Well – I suppose it would, even if you went in to Green Bay to mail them. But – are you going to take the chance of staying out there tonight? Everything that's happened has been, or has started, along that road you live on. And the last thing, the cat, right where you live!'

Doc smiled. 'I'll be all right tonight, Miss Talley,' he told her.

And he was, because the mind thing was otherwise occupied.

CHAPTER SEVENTEEN

The mind thing, finally freed of his annoying imprisonment in a host that had become of no further use to him, was back in his own body, his own shell, under the back steps of the Gross farmhouse. He felt relieved and well satisfied with what he had just done. He had taken his cat-host so far into the woods before drowning it that its body would probably never be found. Staunton might wonder if he learned that the cat had not returned to its former home – but Staunton would never learn that because tonight, while he slept, he would cease to *be* Staunton; the mind thing would have him.

The mind thing's plans were simple, and he'd had plenty of time to think them out while, as a cat, he'd nothing to do but laze around Staunton's house and play the cat role to the hilt. He felt sure that he'd done just that; he'd managed not to do a single thing out of character for a cat. He'd been tempted, just for a second, when Staunton had offered to shoot him – but he'd seen through the trap easily. If he'd gone to sit on the target on the floor, Staunton's suspicions would have been verified and shooting him would have been the *last* thing Staunton would have done. Instead, Staunton would probably have caged him and kept him indefinitely for intensive study. Possibly he'd even have fed him intravenously by force to keep him from achieving death by starvation.

But all that was safely past now, and after tonight he'd be really safe. He'd be in control of the only human being who was a menace to him and who at the same time was his optimum host.

It was of such major importance that he take over Staunton at the earliest possible time that he wouldn't even take the risk of using an animal or bird host for the purpose. Mrs Gross would be safer and surer. He'd take her over as soon as she went to sleep. He'd wait until, say, one o'clock, by which time everyone between here and Staunton's place would certainly be sound asleep; then he'd have her carry him that distance. If there was a light on in Staunton's place, she'd wait until a full hour after it had gone out, then hide him within range of the sleeping Staunton. Then she'd come back home and die. He'd make it look like an accident – a fall down the stairs, perhaps, in the middle of the night. True, her death, in any way except a natural one, would be a suspicious coincidence so shortly after her husband's death, but that wouldn't matter, because within a minute after her death he'd have Staunton, the one person who could otherwise be dangerous to him. Let others wonder; he'd be safe.

He threw out his preceptor sense to refamiliarise himself with what was currently happening – what changes, if any, might have occurred during the days while his mind had been away.

Mrs Gross was alone in the house, in the kitchen, at the moment sterilising some mason jars in preparation for preserving or canning something.

Nothing had changed in the barnyard or in the barn except that the three cows were no longer in the latter. No doubt they were out in pasture. All was well.

Mrs Gross came out of the house– walking right over him as she came down the kitchen steps. With mild curiosity, and since he had nothing else to do, he followed her with his sense of perception. She went around behind the barn, stopping just about at the limit of his ability to follow her. 'Jim!' she called out, 'Yoo-hoo, Jim!' He heard a voice call back in answer, although it was too far for him to hear the words.

He remembered now. The Kramer boy, he'd learned from conversations in the Gross house, had been willing, at his father's suggestion, to come over and work for Mrs Gross for the rest of the school vacation, or until she had sold the farm and turned it over to the new owner.

He knew and could picture Jim – with the memories of the cat Jerry, which had been a Kramer cat: a husky young boy about the age of Tommy Hoffman. He'd be a much better host than the aging and frail Mrs Gross. But of course he wouldn't be sleeping here.

'Will you bring in a few ears of the corn, Jim?' Mrs Gross was calling out. 'I'll cook it for our lunch, huh? And maybe some cucumbers when you pass the patch.'

She came around the barn and went back into the house.

Jim Kramer stopped what he was doing, picking beans, and mopped his forehead with a handkerchief as he headed for the edge of the cornfield. He was husky all right, and just Tommy's age, and had known Tommy, although they hadn't been really close friends. One way in which they had differed was that Tommy had been interested in farming, would have been content to have spent the rest of his life as a farmer. Jim had bigger ideas. When he'd be graduated in June of next year, he was going to go to college and study engineering. Just what kind he hadn't fully decided yet. Probably mechanical engineering; chemical engineering, his alternative, would perhaps take him further and lead to bigger money, but he was a natural-born mechanic and more interested in machinery than in chemicals, so it would make more sense for him to study something at which he already had a good start. He could take apart and put together any car or tractor he'd ever had a chance to fiddle with, and after college he'd be able to design cars and other machinery.

Meanwhile, he didn't mind farm work and was good at it.

He was glad this deal with Mrs Gross had come along to let him earn some money this summer to add to his college fund. The pay wasn't generous, but it was adequate. And it was a full-time job while it lasted. At first he'd tried – it had been his father's idea – to spend only half of each day here, the other half back on his own farm. But after only a day or two it became obvious that, unless the Gross farm was to deteriorate and lose crops, it was a full-time job. His father had seen the point, and agreed.

He picked half a dozen of the best ears of corn – and then, after considering, two more. He had a healthy appetite and doing outdoor work sharpened it. Mrs Gross would probably eat only two ears, but he might want six himself. On his way to the farmhouse he also picked half a dozen big cucumbers – more than she'd need, but the extra ones would keep – and came around the barn and into the house with them. He put them down on the kitchen table.

When he turned to leave, Mrs Gross said, 'Wait, Jim. It's almost lunchtime; it won't take me long to cook that corn and everything else is ready except for cutting up a couple of cucumbers. Hardly pay you to go all the way out to those beans and back again. Sit down or lie down and rest a little; you've been working hard.'

'Fine,' he said. 'But in that case let me shuck that corn for you first, though. Then maybe I'll take a short nap in the barn till you call me.'

'Barn? Why the barn when there's a nice sofa in the next room? And it'll be easier for me to call you there than having to go out to the barn.'

'Well, all right.'

He shucked the corn for her and then went into the living-room and lay down on the sofa, after taking his shoes off so he wouldn't get it dirty. He wasn't really tired this early in the day, but a fifteen- or twenty-minute nap would be welcome. He was one of those fortunate people who can go to sleep easily and quickly anywhere at any time and awake fully refreshed after even a ten-minute nap.

He closed his eyes and slept – and, in his mind, there was sudden pain and sudden but very brief struggle.

He continued to lie there – but in his brain the mind thing was taking advantage of the rest of the nap period to sort through his memories and readying himself to *be*, or seem to be, Jim Kramer. For the rest of today. He wouldn't have to use the frail German hausfrau after all.

'Ready, Jim,' Mrs Gross called from the kitchen. 'You awake?'

'Sure,' he called back. 'Just a sec.' He swung his feet off the sofa and bent over to put his shoes back on.

He stood and stretched himself in the doorway to the kitchen. 'Mmmm, smells good,' he said.

'Sit down, sit down. Help yourself while it's hot.'

When he had eaten his fill he went back to work. Finishing picking the beans that were ready took most of the afternoon. Tomorrow they'd have to be taken into town to sell to the trucker who'd take them to the cannery. But, the mind thing knew, not by his present host; Jim Kramer would be dead by tomorrow.

When he had brought the cows in from pasture and milked them, he was through for the day. He went home.

The Jim Kramer who ate dinner with his parents that evening was perhaps a little quieter than usual, but otherwise he seemed perfectly normal. The only uncharacteristic thing about him was the way he spent the evening. After the table had been cleared he took all ten volumes of an encyclopedia from the bookcase and started looking through them, reading an article in one volume and then picking another apparently from some reference or word in the preceding article. His father, walking past the table once, saw him reading under 'Electron' and a second time under 'Radar'.

'Thinking about electrical engineering, Jim, instead of mechanical or chemical?' he asked.

'Just looking up a little on it, Dad,' Jim said over his shoulder. 'Electrical engineering or electronics. Electronics is getting more and more important. Just might be the best bet, if I find it makes sense to me.'

'Could be. Well, you got a year to make up your mind.'

'Yes, but it will make some difference in what subjects I take my last year in high. And school starts next month, so I better make up my mind before then.'

Mr Kramer turned away. 'Okay, Jim. Your decision; you know more about it than I do.'

'Wait a minute, Dad. Can I borrow the truck for a few hours tomorrow morning?'

'I guess so; I won't be using it early. But what about working for Mrs Gross?'

'That's okay. With the truck I can work for her and still do an errand of my own at the same time. Got five bushels of beans I got to take in town and sell tomorrow for her. With the pickup I can make it to Green Bay and back in the same time it'd take me to hitch up her horse and wagon and go to Bartlesville. And I'll get her a better price for them in Green Bay and have a chance to do what I want there.'

'And what's that?'

'Just stop at the library to borrow some books. It's kind of – well, spotty, trying to dig information out of assorted parts of an encyclopedia. One good elementary text on electronics would be a lot better.'

'I can see that. Jim, if you can't find what you want at the library, go to a bookstore. And if they haven't got it, have them order it. I'll pay for it. For several books, if you want.'

'Thanks a million, Dad. I think the library will do it, but if it doesn't, I'll take you up on that.'

He gathered up the volumes of the encyclopedia and put them back in the bookcase. The mind within the mind of

Jim Kramer had instantly memorised every page which Jim had apparently only glanced at, in addition to those he had pretended to read. At leisure later, he could digest and evaluate what he had learned.

For the rest of the evening he stayed in character by turning on the radio and listening to it while he read, or appeared to read, the subscription copy of *Popular Mechanics* which had come in the mail that day. At ten o'clock when his parents went up to bed he turned down the radio but kept on reading for a while. Jim had managed to convince his parents that he didn't need quite as much sleep as they did and, since he got up at the same time, it was all right for him to stay up half an hour or an hour longer than they did. At ten-thirty he raided the refrigerator for a snack, as usual, and then went upstairs to his own bedroom. But not to sleep; he took off only his shoes and lay quietly on top of his bed until the luminous dial of his wrist-watch told him it was half past two. Then he left very quietly, carrying his shoes till he was safe outside the house.

There was bright moonlight, both an advantage and a danger, since he could see easily himself, but also could be seen. When he died tomorrow morning in an auto accident on the way to Green Bay – and the mind thing had decided to wait that long; there was no logical way for him to die accidentally tonight without causing speculation and investigation – the mind thing did not want anyone to report having seen him abroad tonight. Quickly and quietly he made his way to the Gross farm, reached under the kitchen steps and dug briefly, bringing out the shell that was the material body, now deserted, of the thing that now animated Jim Kramer. He smoothed back the dirt so there would be no indication that anything had been buried there.

With the shell inside his shirt, so that if he *were* seen it would not be reported that he had been carrying something, he started back past his own house and towards Staunton's. Twice he made detours off the road and into the woods; two of the intervening farms had watchdogs that would bark if he went by on the road, perhaps waking someone who might look out of a window and see him.

The house at the end of the road was dark; Staunton was in bed and probably asleep. But in case he might be lying awake, Jim took off his shoes for the trip across the yard and around the house. There were steps leading up to the kitchen door here too, and it would be as good a hiding place as any. He buried the shell again, this time being even more careful than at the Gross place to smooth over the dirt and leave no indication of digging and burying.

Then he went back home by the same route, let himself in quietly and tiptoed upstairs to his bedroom. Mission accomplished. This time he undressed down to his shorts, because his mother would look in to waken him in the morning and that was the way he had been sleeping. Deliberately he tossed and turned enough to rumple the sheets thoroughly, and then lay quietly until his mother opened the door and called him. He answered sleepily and sat up on the edge of the bed yawning.

At breakfast he still acted sleepy and yawned a few times. When his mother asked if he'd stayed up later than usual last night he told her that he hadn't, but that for some reason he'd had trouble getting to sleep, hadn't really slept soundly until maybe an hour or so before she'd wakened him.

'Probably worrying about this career decision you're considering,' his father said. 'But, Jim, if you got only an hour or two of sleep, I don't like the idea of your driving into Green Bay; you might go to sleep at the wheel. Why don't you go back to bed, and let me tell Mrs Gross you'll be able to work only a half day today? She won't mind for once and you can make that trip this afternoon instead.'

Jim yawned again. 'Thanks, Dad, but no; I'll be all right

as soon as I start working and get wakened up. I'll just turn in earlier tonight to make up for it. I'm okay.'

Half an hour later he was through Bartlesville and on the way to Green Bay. He had let Mrs Gross catch him yawning too, while he loaded the beans into the pickup truck. With both his parents and Mrs Gross able to testify to how sleepy he was, there wouldn't be any question, when he ran off the road into a tree or swerved into a head-on collision with another car, of suicide – of anything but his having gone to sleep at the wheel.

He decided finally on a concrete bridge abutment he knew he'd be reaching in another ten miles or so. A swerve head-on into another car would provide even more impact, but would involve someone else's death besides his own. So that was discarded, not out of any feeling of mercy for the other victims – human lives meant nothing at all to the mind thing – but simply because it would make the accident more spectacular, more talked about.

The bridge abutment came, and he hit it squarely, at a little over sixty miles an hour. The impact was sufficient.

Instantly the mind thing was back in his own body, now under the back steps of the house Staunton was living in.

It was five minutes after nine o'clock.

CHAPTER EIGHTEEN

Doc Staunton had slept fitfully, not over the equivalent of two or three hours during the night, and when he awakened at seven and saw that it was light, he gave up trying to sleep.

He made himself breakfast and then sat over coffee waiting till it got late enough to go to town. He and Miss Talley had talked quite a while over dinner and he doubted that she'd finished his typing before midnight, or even later; he knew he shouldn't call at her house before nine at the earliest, and ten would be better. He was restless, though, and at eight-thirty he got into the station wagon and drove into town.

There was nothing to do when he got there. He didn't want to go to the post office or call the sheriff before he'd got the statements from Miss Talley and, even if he'd felt like having a beer so early in the morning, the tavern didn't open until ten. He stopped in the restaurant for more coffee.

At a quarter after nine, he decided he'd still wait fifteen minutes to call Miss Talley and see if she was up and ready to see him. By now the sheriff should be in his office in Wilcox; he could call there now and try to make an appointment for later in the morning.

He got the sheriff on the wire and was just getting around to setting the time for an appointment when the sheriff said, 'Just a second, Doc. Hold the line.' And then, a minute later, 'Doc, it can't be this morning; you'll have to call me later.

Just got a flash from a state police radio car. There's been an accident between Bartlesville and Green Bay; got to get there quick. Sorry.' The line went dead.

Doc replaced the receiver and stared for a moment at the phone, wondering whether the accident could possibly have happened to anyone he knew. Probably not, he thought, or the sheriff would have mentioned it – but then again the sheriff didn't know exactly who Doc knew, except for a few people; and besides, the sheriff had been in a hurry.

He dropped another coin and called the sheriff's office. When a deputy answered, Doc identified himself and explained that he'd been talking to the sheriff when an accident flash had caused the sheriff to excuse himself; could the deputy tell him who, if anyone, had been hurt in the accident?

The deputy was co-operative. A high school student named James Kramer, who lived somewhere outside Bartlesville, had been killed. He'd been alone in a truck he was driving to Green Bay and he'd probably gone to sleep at the wheel; he'd driven straight into a concrete bridge abutment and had died instantly.

Doc thanked him and had hung up again before the name Kramer began to register. It was a family named Kramer who lived next to Mrs Gross, and he remembered now having heard that their son, a high school boy about Tommy Hoffman's age, had been working for Mrs Gross until she could sell her farm. And the Kramers had owned the grey cat that had spent almost a week with him – until yesterday!

And now the Kramer boy was dead – under circumstances that could all too easily have been suicide. Human suicide number three, and again a connection between it and an animal suicide!

Suddenly, Doc Staunton wasn't scared any more. He felt coldly calm, knowing what he had to do – and quickly, since he'd wasted too much time already.

This – whatever *this* was – was nothing for a county sheriff. This was something for investigation by the FBI and by top scientists. Not that he wouldn't talk to the sheriff too, but this was way over the heads of local law enforcement officers, even of the state police – although the FBI would want to use them for routine parts of the investigation. Maybe he could even get the army interested. Fortunately he knew, from his work on satellite and moon-probe projects, several top army security officers and two FBI men. More to the point, they knew *him* well enough not to dismiss him as a crackpot and to give serious consideration to anything, however seemingly wild and impossible, that he told them.

He'd start phoning people, and stirring things up, the moment he got those statements from Miss Talley. But one thing came ahead even of that, something he could do right now that would take him less than an hour: Move out of the danger zone.

He was already walking to his car as he decided that. He'd go out to the house, pack his belongings and put them in the station wagon. Then, when he picked up Miss Talley's typing, he'd head right for Green Bay, make his headquarters at a hotel there, and start making long-distance calls. If he had half as much influence as he thought he had, there'd be FBI men and security agents in town before the day was over. And while he was waiting for them he could find out as much as possible about the death of Jim Kramer and add that to his statement. A Green Bay stenographer could take care of that, unless Miss Talley wanted to go to Green Bay with him and follow through with what she'd started. He rather thought that she would.

The mind thing's first sweep with his perceptor sense told him that Staunton was not at home. This was mildly surprising, at a few minutes after nine in the morning; Staunton seldom went into town that early. Nor had he gone fishing or for a walk, because the car was gone too. Still—

The mind thing checked. All of Staunton's personal possessions were still there, except the clothes he'd been wearing. Dishes in the sink and other evidence showed that he'd had breakfast. He must have awakened earlier than usual and decided, for whatever reason, to take an early trip into town instead of going at his usual time, which was late morning or early afternoon. Nothing to worry about; he'd be back. And unless by fortunate circumstance he should take a nap today, then tonight—

Although, as a cat, he had spent several days and nights in this house, he had – in that form – been deprived of his perceptor sense. He couldn't see into closed rooms or closets, couldn't read closed books or folded letters. Now, at leisure, he could remedy those omissions, and he did.

For future reference – since, once he'd taken over Staunton as a host, he'd no longer be free to use his perception, but would have to depend upon the human being's relatively limited sense organs – he memorised the house and everything that was in it. Even with Staunton as host, he'd be here at least another week or two. Just how long he wouldn't know until he discovered the factors he'd find in Staunton's thoughts and memories. But it would be too suspicious to have his host leave immediately and suddenly, since his plans were apparently to stay the rest of the summer.

He felt the vibrations of the car approaching before it came within range of his perception. It was Staunton's station wagon and Staunton was in it alone. It was ten by the kitchen clock.

As Staunton came to the front door and let himself in, the mind thing, just to complete his inventory, used his perceptive sense on the car Staunton had just left. Suddenly, for the first time, he realised that something must have gone wrong. Carefully rolled up in an old tarpaulin was the dead, drowned body of a small grey cat. His second-last host. How had Staunton discovered it, and why did he now have it in his car? Had he been trailed through the woods to the stream? He'd never thought of that possibility, but he *must* have been. He'd been satisfied to look back at the house and to see that he wasn't being followed by sight. But that brief sprinkle of rain – of course, he'd left paw prints that Staunton had managed to follow. Again he'd given himself away.

Well, Staunton was back home now, and sooner or later he'd sleep. And after that, whatever he'd suspected wouldn't matter.

But what was Staunton doing now? He was getting his two suitcases from the storage room and carrying them upstairs, putting his clothes in them, packing his razor and other things from the bathroom. *He was packing to leave, and permanently, since he was taking everything.*

But he couldn't; he had to be stopped, at any cost.

Doc Staunton carried the suitcases out to the station wagon and put them in the back, then returned to the house. He made one quick round of it, closing all the windows and making sure that the back door was locked. In the kitchen he hesitated whether to flick the switch that would shut off the gasoline engine and generator in the basement, and then decided not to. There was still food in the refrigerator and it wouldn't spoil for a few days. And he'd be back, although not alone and not to stay here; but he'd certainly be showing the place to whoever would be in charge of the investigation. He might as well leave the current on.

That took care of everything except his fishing equipment, guns, and ammunition in the storage room. Using the creel to carry the boxes of cartridges and shells, he carried it and the other fishing equipment, including his high boots, out to the station wagon and then came back for the three guns – the pistol, the rifle, and the over-and-under shotgun.

That was all, and he pocketed the pistol and held the two guns under one arm to give him a free hand to lock the front door behind him and pocket the key. Then he started for the station wagon.

He was almost there, just reaching for the door handle, when he saw the deer, a six-point buck. It was standing, with no attempt at concealing itself, about fifty feet away, at the edge of the woods, just past the point where the road started ouside his yard. It stared back at him, then lowered its head and pawed the earth, readying itself for a charge.

Quickly he got inside the car and started the engine. He had a sudden hunch as to what was coming, but there was only one way to find out. He put the car in gear and started it. He'd have to drivc right past the buck, within a few yards of it, to get away – if the buck would let him.

The buck wasn't going to let him. It started its charge the moment the car started to move. He braked to a stop and even tried – but didn't have time – to reduce the impact by getting the car moving in reverse. Head down, the buck was a two-hundred-pound missile that hit the radiator dead centre, between the headlights, and then the buck was two hundred pounds of dead deer with broken antlers, broken skull, broken neck. The car had moved backward almost two feet and only Doc's final split-second move of throwing himself down sidewise across the front seat saved him from having at least a sore neck from the whiplash effect he'd have experienced had he remained sitting upright.

He sat up slowly. The engine had died, or had been killed by the backward motion of the car while it was still in a forward gear. He turned off the ignition; he didn't try to re-start the car. He knew it would never run again until it had been towed to a garage and equipped, at the very minimum, with a new radiator and a new fan. It wouldn't have surprised him if other damage had been done, possibly even a cracked block.

The rifle, being only a .22, would be useless, and even with a pistol and a shotgun he'd never make it afoot to town, or even to the nearest farmhouse that had a telephone, if a series of animal hosts was to be sent against him. Not past fields, on one side of the road, that contained cows and maybe even a few bulls drowsing in the shade of trees. And on the other side of the road, a long stretch of virgin woodland that certainly contained more deer, possibly even a bear or two, and wildcats. There was an even nastier possibility than any one of these: what if the enemy could find a human host taking a midday nap? What could he possibly do if Mrs Kramer, say, or Mrs Gross should come out to the road with a shotgun or rifle and start shooting at him? Shoot back? Of course it wouldn't really be a *sane* Mrs Kramer or Mrs Gross doing the shooting – but even so, he knew he wouldn't be able to shoot a woman. And no matter how many animals or humans he might succeed in killing on the way to get help, sooner or later someone or something would manage to kill him instead. He knew, or felt fairly sure, that there was only one *mind* against him – but it was a mind that could send a practically endless succession of attackers against him, more than he could hope to handle.

Well, he reflected, at least the cold war is over. The enemy – whatever it was – was no longer pretending. At least from him, Doc Staunton, it would make no further attempt to conceal its powers. It wanted to keep him here, and it could. He reached into the back seat for the creel and loaded the shotgun and the pistol, and stuffed all the extra cartridges for the former and shells for the latter into various pockets.

Strangely, he wasn't scared at all. He was even more coldly calm, calmly analytical. And he knew that he would have to be if he was to stand a chance to win this war. If he was to win it, his mind would have to be his major weapon; firearms might win a battle, but never the war.

First, immediate survival. Would he be safer here in the

car than back in the house? He thought he would be just as safe and much more comfortable, especially for an extended siege, back in the house. The enemy had served notice that it would kill him to keep him from reaching help. But would the enemy try to kill him anyway, even if he accepted the state of siege and didn't try to leave?

He couldn't be sure, but one thing had been a strong indication that the enemy was not trying to kill him unless again he tried to leave. If the enemy wanted his immediate death, he'd probably be dead already. He hadn't noticed the deer standing there until he had almost reached the car, but it had been watching him. It could have charged sooner than it did – and at him instead of at the car. And none of the guns had been loaded then.

So, the house. He got out of the car cautiously, the pistol in a pocket and the shotgun at ready, and looked about him. Nothing alive was in sight. Unless—

He looked upwards. About a hundred feet in the air a wild duck was wheeling in slow circles – as a buzzard circles. A duck does not fly that way. Air attack? He hadn't thought of that when he had been considering the dangers of trying to reach town afoot, but he saw now that a kamikaze attack from the air by any reasonably heavy bird would be fully as dangerous as, say, a charge by a maddened cow or horse. He kept a wary eye on the circling duck as he started for the house. Suddenly, when he was about halfway, it dived. He jerked up the gun ready to fire and then leap aside – but he didn't have to. The bird wasn't dive-bombing *him*, but a point in the yard, a dozen or so yards away from him; it hit the ground with a sickening thud that raised a cloud of dust and probably made a dent in the hard-packed soil of the yard.

Thoughtfully, Doc let himself into the house and locked the door. No, the enemy was not trying to kill him, only to keep him penned here. The dive of the duck couldn't possibly have missed him by that much if it had been aimed at him. The enemy had done it merely to give him a demonstration of the futility of his trying to escape afoot by showing him, in case he hadn't thought of it (as he hadn't at first), one more deadly means of preventing his escape. The wild duck could as easily have dived at him as not; it had nothing to lose since it was making a suicidal plunge in any case. Therefore: the enemy did not *want* him dead, as long as it could keep him here instead.

He reloaded the upper barrel of the shotgun and leaned it against the window beside the front door. He emptied his pockets of the extra shells and cartridges and put them on the end of the sofa, in easy reach. Then he sat down on the arm of the sofa, facing the window and looking out.

Nothing moved outside. Was he imagining things? Would it be safe for him to leave and walk to town? No, if the deer hadn't been proof enough, then the plummeting duck had been the convincer.

There was no attack now, and he didn't think there would be, as long as he stayed here and made no attempt to leave. But why?

He started for the refrigerator to get himself a bottle of beer, but changed his mind and came back. Beer, in moderation, wouldn't impair much his ability to think. Still, even a trifling impairment might make all the difference.

What was the nature of the enemy? Human, possibly mutant, with a hitherto undemonstrated psi ability of being able to take over other minds? Demon? Alien? Somehow, the last seemed least unlikely of the three; as Miss Talley had pointed out, there are billions of habitable worlds in the universe; why shouldn't life and intelligence have developed on some of them? Why should Earth be unique? And why couldn't some intelligent life form have developed some form of space travel? Why should human beings be the first to do so?

Yes, definitely it seemed more possible than the only alternatives he could think of – and more dangerous.

But why was he now being singled out for attack? Because he now knew and suspected enough to be dangerous to the enemy? Yes, he was; regardless of how the enemy (keep calling it that, he decided, regardless of what he or it really was) knew about it.

Of course, he realised: using the grey cat as host, it had spent over five days with him. It had heard what he'd dictated to Miss Talley and knew that he planned to mail the statements he'd dictated to important friends. And it had studied *him* all the time he'd kept it captive – to study it.

Yes, he was dangerous to the enemy, and the enemy knew it. But why, then, hadn't the enemy killed him? With the deer, it could have easily, simply by charging before he got into the car instead of after. And, with the dive-bombing duck, it hadn't even tried; the dive into the ground hadn't been a serious attempt to hit him. The enemy wanted him alive, but here, not elsewhere. Why?

Because it wanted him for a host? It seemed a possible answer, but why didn't it take him as one, or try to?

Nothing was happening outside, and he went into the kitchen and put water on the stove to boil for coffee. Was some special circumstance necessary for the enemy to take over a host?

Suddenly he thought of a possible answer, and the more he thought about it the more possible it seemed. Tommy Hoffman had been taken over while he was sleeping. So had Siegfried Gross. It was less certain that Jim Kramer had been sleeping, but he could have been. And the animal hosts: almost all animals – and especially cats and dogs – sleep frequently, if briefly, by day as well as by night.

But if the enemy was keeping him here until he slept, so he could be taken over, then why hadn't he been taken over last night? He'd not slept well, but off and on he had slept a little. Then the answer, or at least *an* answer, came to him. For whatever reason, after the death of the grey cat, the enemy had taken the Kramer boy as his next host – and had, this time, waited until he could make the boy's death seem an accident rather than a suicide. Which was another proof, or at least an indication, that the enemy was singular, not plural, and could operate only one host at a time. If he could only be sure—

Making his mind up suddenly, Doc picked up the shotgun and went to the door and opened it, took a cautious step out on to the small unroofed porch and looked up.

Birds, big birds, were circling up in the sky, six or seven of them. Birds, plural. Had he been wrong?

Then relief came to him as he watched them for a moment and saw them more clearly. These birds were not hosts; they were buzzards circling over the dead deer, circling slowly down for a carrion feast. Ordinary birds. Never before had buzzards seemed beautiful to him; they did in that moment.

Then, from the direction of the woods, he saw another bird coming; it looked like another duck. As it came nearer it flew higher to gain altitude and then started a dive, straight towards him. He could probably have shot it by throwing up the shotgun, but there was no point in taking the risk. He stepped back inside quickly and closed the door. A second later there was the loud thud of its crash-landing on to the boards of porch.

Doc smiled grimly; by taking the slight risk he had taken in stepping outside he thought that he had verified at least one of his deductions. If the enemy could take over a creature which was awake it could easily have taken over one of those big circling buzzards already in the sky, much closer. Or all of them, if it could manage more than one host at a time. Instead, it had had to lose time by finding a bird farther away, a bird that was sleeping, probably.

Dangerous as the enemy could be, it must have limitations.

There was hope, then. Miss Talley was expecting him; sooner or later she'd get worried enough to call the sheriff. If the sheriff started for this place and didn't get through alive, that would be tough on the sheriff; but other officers would follow to see what happened to him, and if they were attacked the state police would get on the job. A *group* of armed men could get through anything the enemy could throw against them, one animal at a time.

Yes, help would come, eventually. His main problem would be to stay awake till then.

CHAPTER NINETEEN

For what seemed an eternity, nothing happened. Night fell, the time for sleep. Doc went around the house, upstairs and down, turning on the lights, all of the lights.

And then the lights went out, all together.

The generator? Of course the generator. The gasoline motor that ran it was not out of fuel; there was enough in the tank to run it for several more days. But either the generator or the motor that ran it had stopped.

The enemy had taken another host. A mouse? Probably a mouse – a domestic mouse if there were any in the cellar; otherwise a field mouse that had been taken over and directed to find a way in somehow, had got through the housing of the gasoline engine or the motor that it ran, and that mouse would now be dead, smeared around a commutator perhaps . . . And there was no use trying to restart the engine or the generator – there were more mice wherever the first one had come from. Or perhaps it had not been a mouse at all. Even an insect, directed by an intelligent mind, can so place itself as to die in the process of shorting a motor or a generator.

Darkness.

Above all, he must fight getting sleepy. Sleep would be the end.

A moon came up. It was only a three-quarter moon but it was bright in a clear, starry sky. He could see outside the house now, in all directions. And enough moonlight came in the front windows so he could see fairly well in the living-room – well enough to pace without risking falling over anything. He had a flashlight, but even with the one extra battery he had for it, it wasn't going to last the whole night; he would have to use it sparingly.

How long would he be able to stay awake? Another twenty-four hours, he thought, despite the fact that he'd slept so little the night before and already felt tired.

He was getting hungry, too, but he decided not to eat anything. Food can tend to make one sleepy, especially when one is already tired before eating. A hungry man can stay awake more easily than a full one – at least up to the point where starvation or malnutrition weakens him. That wouldn't happen here; he knew that he could go without food for a much longer period than he could go without sleep.

He paced, thought, tried to think harder. Somehow he had to counter-attack. But how?'

In what way was the enemy vulnerable? Was it incorporeal or did it have a body of its own – perhaps dormant while it was using a host? He thought it must have a body: first, because he found it almost impossible to think of an incorporeal entity; second, because he was remembering now one strange thing in connection with the suicide of Siegfried Gross. A jar of meat stock and a bowl of gravy had disappeared from Elsa Gross's refrigerator that night. Gross would hardly have eaten them in that form; and he would have had no reason to pour them down the sink. But they were prime ingredients for a nutrient solution that should feed anyone or anything with a bodily chemistry remotely similar to that of a terrestrial creature. Had Gross been taken as a host for the purpose of feeding the enemy before killing himself? It sounded grotesque, yes – but what, in everything that had been happening, did *not* sound grotesque? It seemed at least possible.

He went out to the kitchen and made as brief use as possible of the flashlight to make another pot of coffee. When it was ready he returned with a cup of it and again sat on the arm of the sofa staring out into the bright moonlight.

Where would the enemy's body be? Quite probably, since there must be some limit to the range at which it could operate, it was nearby; this house was the focus of the attack. Quite possibly within sight of the house; conceivably even inside it. He didn't think the enemy would have taken that chance, but the fact that it might have did open up one possible line of counter-offensive. Not tonight, but as soon as it was light tomorrow, he'd search the inside of the house thoroughly, ready to shoot anything alive that he found.

It was a long, long night, and the lonesomest night he'd ever spent. But it *did* end.

When it was light enough, he searched the house thoroughly, room by room, and then the basement. He didn't know, of course, what he was looking for, or how small or how large an object it might be, but unless the enemy had the ability to disguise itself as a small household object, or to become invisible, both of which he doubted, he convinced himself that it wasn't there. In the basement he found that his guess about the generator had been right. Something like a mouse had crawled into it through the housing and was now nothing more than a red smear. He could have cleaned it and started it again, but to what purpose? If the enemy didn't want him to have electricity, another small something would stop either the generator or the motor the moment he went back upstairs.

Only one other possibility had come to him during the endless night. Since the enemy was the helpless prisoner, in a sense, of any host he took, and could escape to take another host only with the death of the current one, then there was one way in which he, Doc, might have a chance to turn the tables. If he could slightly wound and capture, or capture without wounding, whatever host might be used against him next – and keep that host alive under circumstances in which it could not bring about its own death, then the enemy would be helpless for a while. And that might be perhaps long enough to let him get into town alive and safe.

But would he have such a chance?

He stared up at the ceiling and felt sudden hope when he saw a moth flying around up there. Could it be? A moth was not dangerous in any way, but maybe the enemy was controlling it – was using the moth as a spy to keep closer track of him than could be done otherwise.

Casually he got up and strolled into the storage room, closing the door behind him. He went to work quickly and made a very crude butterfly net. He bent a coathanger into an approximate circle. He ripped apart a sleeping bag to get the piece of cheesecloth that was a part of it, the part that could be propped up over the head to keep insects away, and fastened it around the wire loop made from the coathanger. He managed to tie this on to the end of a broom handle. It looked like a far cry from a real butterfly net, but it might serve the purpose of one.

The moth was still circling. It took several passes, but he got it. He took it out of the net very carefully so as not to injure even a wing. Then, in the kitchen, he found a box of kitchen matches and emptied it; he put the moth inside and closed the lid. The moth would live for a while, long enough for him to make his getaway. That is, if the moth was—

He might as well find out right away, he decided. Getting the shotgun, he opened the front door and stepped through it, looked around and saw nothing to be frightened of. Not even in the air above.

He took a deep breath and started walking. He got only about ten paces before something made him look upwards again. A chicken hawk, a big one, had just taken off from the eaves of the house and was rising to circle. It dived at him, and it was aiming to kill, not just to frighten him back into the house.

He got the shotgun up just in time and pulled the trigger when the chicken hawk was only eight or ten feet over his head and coming like the guided missile it was. Blood and feathers flew, some right into his face. The rest of what was left of the bird, knocked out of its straight-line trajectory, hit the ground only two feet away from him.

He ran back for the house. He washed the blood and feathers off his face and brushed his clothes. Then he opened the kitchen matchbox and released the moth – the moth that was only a moth, and not a host of the enemy. His idea had been a good one, but the enemy hadn't intended to give him that simple a way of winning.

CHAPTER TWENTY

And then – nothing happened.

Minutes dragged by like hours. He had by now not slept for a little over twenty-four hours; and, because of his wakefulness, had slept not longer than three hours out of the preceding twenty-four.

Most of the time he walked from window to window, looking out at – nothing. His legs ached with weariness and he would have given a thousand dollars just to be able to lie down a few minutes to rest, but it was too dangerous. He didn't even dare to sit down comfortably and lean back. When he did sit, it was either on the arm of the sofa, looking out of the front window, or on the edge of a chair in the kitchen. From time to time he drank a cup of coffee, but now he drank it cold; he had realised some time ago that the soporific effect of drinking a bulk of hot liquid at least partially counteracted the effect of the caffeine.

The morning crawled along. Surely the sheriff or the state police would come; surely Miss Talley, no later than this morning, would have notified one or the other, would have told someone that he had failed to keep an appointment with her yesterday and might be in trouble or in danger.

He couldn't stay awake much longer. Now it was getting dangerous even for him to sit; he'd find his eyes starting to go shut and would have to force them open again. And although ordinarily he was only a moderate smoker, he'd been smoking his pipe so much that his mouth felt raw. Benzedrine would have been worth its weight in diamonds to him, but he had brought none with him; one doesn't think of having to stay awake when on vacation.

It was almost noon, and he was standing at the front window, wishing, but not daring, at least to lean his forehead against the pane, when he heard the sound of an approaching car.

He picked up the shotgun and opened the front door, but stood just inside, ready to cover the sheriff, or whoever it was, against attack from whatever direction.

Then the car turned into the yard. A tiny car, a Volkswagen – and Miss Talley was in it, alone.

He made frantic motions waving her away, hoping that if she turned and left quickly—

But she drove on in, not looking towards him because her attention was distracted by the sight of his station wagon and the dead deer – from which buzzards rose lazily and flapped away as the car came near them. She'd shut off her engine before she looked towards the door and saw him.

'Miss Talley!' he called to her. 'Turn around and get back to town, fast. Get the state police and—'

It wasn't any use. He heard hoofbeats – a bull was charging down the road, only a hundred feet away. The Volkswagen was only a dozen feet from Doc, and suddenly he saw a chance, if a dangerous one, to win. If he could wound the bull without killing it, put it out of action with, say, a broken leg so it couldn't kill itself and free the enemy to take another host—

Calling to Miss Talley to stay in the car, he ran out alongside it and raised the shotgun; if he could judge the distance just right and shoot low, hoping to hit the front legs—

His aim was good, but excitement made him shoot a little too soon. The charge hurt the bull, but didn't stop it. It bellowed in rage and changed direction, coming straight for him instead of for the Volkswagen. By the time he shot the second barrel it was too close, only ten feet away; the shot had to be fatal, and it was. Because of its momentum it kept coming and he had to step aside; it fell dead just beyond him.

He opened the door of the Volkswagen. 'Hurry into the house, Miss Talley. We've got a minute's grace before it can try again, but don't waste any time.'

He hurried with her. The shotgun was empty, and the extra shells were inside. At the door he turned and looked back and upwards. A big bird of some kind, not a buzzard, was circling – but if it was about to attack it was too late. He stepped inside and closed the door.

Quickly, while he was reloading the shotgun, he told her what had happened yesterday and thus far today.

'Oh, Doctor,' she said, 'if I'd only insisted that the sheriff— I called him yesterday afternoon and he didn't seem to believe you were in trouble but he said he'd come out. I couldn't reach him again until this morning, and then he told me several things had come up, that he hadn't been able to make it yesterday and wouldn't be able to until tomorrow. I guess he thought it was just my imagination that anything could be wrong, and he isn't in any hurry.'

'Tomorrow . . .' Doc shook his head gloomily. 'I'll never make it – stay awake that long, I mean. And if I'm right that as soon as I go to sleep— I wish you hadn't come yourself, Miss Talley; now you're in trouble too.'

'Don't you think there's even a chance of our making it into town in my car? With me driving so you can use the gun?'

'A chance in a hundred, Miss Talley. Aside from the fact that there must be cows wherever that bull came from, not to mention more deer in the woods, I'll bet a really big bird could dive-bomb right through the roof of a light car like that. How soon will you be missed? Will neighbours notice that you don't get home tonight, if you don't?'

'Oh, dear, I'm afraid not. Every once in a while I go in to Green Bay to see a show and I have a sister-in-law there who goes with me and I usually stay with her afterwards. So no one will think anything of my not getting home tonight, because my neighbours know that, and won't worry. Oh, if I'd only thought of calling the state police instead of coming myself – I never thought of them at all.'

Doc Staunton gestured wearily. 'Don't blame yourself for anything, Miss Talley. *I* made the first mistake – the first *two* mistakes. I should never have stayed here the night before last, after the grey cat killed itself; that made this house, or at least this area, a focus. And yesterday morning, after I learned about Jim Kramer's death, I should never have come back here just to pack up my possessions. That was the big mistake, the one that caught me.' He sighed.

'Let's have some coffee. I've been drinking it cold, but now that I have someone to talk to, I think I'll risk a cup of it hot. I'll even risk sitting down and letting you make it – if you'll keep talking to me, or vice versa. Maybe we can come up with something. We've *got* to come up with something.'

In the kitchen he compromised by leaning against the wall while she started water boiling for fresh coffee. He did most of the talking, since he had more to tell.

'The *alien*,' Miss Talley said firmly, the first time he mentioned the enemy. 'Doctor, why not admit we're fighting – or at any rate defending ourselves against – an extraterrestrial intelligence? What else *could* it be?'

'A mutant human being, one who was born with or has acquired what Charles Fort called a wild talent.'

'Do you really believe that?'

'No,' Doc said. 'Nor the only other possibility I've been able to think of – a demon or devil. But I won't narrow it down. Until I know for sure, or until I lose, I'm going to call him the enemy. Let's not worry about nomenclature, Miss Talley. There's too much else to worry about. First and foremost, what chance have we got, if any? Of course I can *hope* I'm wrong in thinking the enemy is keeping me – us, rather – boxed in here until I have to go to sleep.'

'Have you had any ideas at all?'

He told her his thought that wounding an animal controlled by the enemy might give them time for a getaway. 'But,' he added, 'it's hard to wound a large animal with a shotgun in such a way that it couldn't attack, or manage to kill itself. You'd have to break a leg to immobilise it.'

'You don't have a rifle?'

'Only a twenty-two; it's still in the station wagon, and not worth the risk of trying to get it. It would be if I had long rifle cartridges for it, but I have only shorts; I intended to use it only for target practice. I have a pistol, but I'm not accurate enough with it to take the risk of trying to wound a charging animal without killing it.'

He shook his head wearily. 'I think it recognises the risk of being wounded and that's why it prefers to use birds. Even if I could shoot one high enough in the air only to wound it with a few pellets, it would already be diving and the fall would kill it . . . Lord, but I'm sleepy.'

'Is there anything I can do to help?'

'Just keep talking, or listening. By the way, I'm on a hunger strike to keep awake, but don't let that stop you from getting yourself something any time you want. The refrigerator's been off since yesterday evening, so don't take a chance on anything in it. But there's plenty of canned goods.'

The coffee was finished and she poured two cups and brought them to the table. 'Thanks, I'm not hungry yet. But perhaps I should make two or three extra pots of coffee.'

'If you wish. But why?'

'Since he managed to shut off your electricity, he just might figure a way to shut off the gas too. And you don't want to be without coffee, even if both of us will have to drink it cold.'

'I don't think he could, short of using a human host. It takes a wrench to turn the valve on the butane tank. There's nothing to lose, though, if you want to make a couple of extra pots.'

She put more water on the stove to boil and then came to the table and sat across from him.

'How about the water supply? Any chance of his shutting that off? If so, I'd better fill a few buckets, to be safe.'

'I don't think it's necessary.' He explained how the water supply worked. 'He could easily enough wreck the pump that brings water from the well to the tank on the roof, but the tank itself is heavy and solid and it must be at least half full; more water than we'll need. It holds two hundred gallons.'

He took a sip of his coffee.

'Talking about water reminds me of something I'll do when I've finished this. A cold bath and a change of clothes will help me; I should have thought of it this morning, but I didn't.'

'It sounds like a good idea. And I'll get myself something to eat while you're upstairs. You must be pretty hungry, and that way you won't have to watch me eat.'

'Fine. But make a circuit of the windows once in a while and call me if you see anything. I'll take a robe into the bathroom with me so I can come quickly. And that reminds me—'

He started to get up, but Miss Talley, in her best schoolteacher manner, ordered him to sit still and got up to make a circuit of the downstairs windows. She came back to report nothing new except that the buzzards were back at the dead deer. None as yet had gone to the dead bull; the deer was riper and more to their taste.

Doc nodded. 'I don't expect anything to happen. It's a waiting game – unless one of us tries to leave. He's made no attempt to get inside the house, in any form, and if he wanted to he could have, long ago. Any big animal could break through either door, unless I shot it first.'

'Or a human being. I wonder why he hasn't sent one against you.'

'No reason to, unless he wanted to kill me, and apparently he doesn't, unless I try to leave. In a way, I wish he would send one. It's dangerous to try to shoot a leg of a charging bull without killing it. But with a man, it would be relatively easy.'

'Doctor, when I came – how did you know I wasn't – the enemy? You could have shot me in the leg easily enough.'

He laughed. 'It never occurred to me. And if it had, the bull coming right after you would have been proof enough. The thing we're most certain of is that he can't control more than one host at a time.' He stood up and stretched his arms, fighting back a yawn. 'Well, to my cold tub. And I'll make circuits of the upstairs windows while the water's running. You won't have to, until after you hear it stop.'

He went upstairs, and half an hour later he came back down, looking at least outwardly refreshed. Miss Talley had finished eating and they sat in the living-room and took turns talking. Doc insisted on making periodic rounds of the windows himself instead of letting her do it. He explained that the danger of his going to sleep if she left him alone was a more important factor than his doing an occasional bit of walking.

The hours dragged. One or the other of them thought of a dozen things to try, but for one reason or another had to reject each as impractical or too dangerous. Once Doc verified that the siege was still on by stepping outside with the shotgun. When he saw a high-circling bird start a dive, he fired at it without waiting for it to get close. But if any of the pellets hit and wounded it, the wound was insufficient to deflect it and he had to use the second barrel when it was dangerously close. Even then he had to jump back the instant he fired or the bird would have hit him. It thudded against the doorsill. He reloaded the shotgun before using its muzzle to push the dead bird – it was, or had been, a chicken hawk – off the porch.

Blood had spattered on his shoes and the cuffs of his trousers. He went upstairs to change them and to take another cold bath; he'd left the water in the tub, since he'd realized while taking the first one that even the hundred gallons that he estimated had been in the tank wouldn't fill the tub too many times. The second bath didn't help much; in fact, he almost went to sleep in the tub and he realised that he was almost at the limit of his ability to stay awake.

When he came downstairs he told Miss Talley so, and asked her to bring in a pan of cold water and a glass, and to keep the glass filled, or half filled, from the pan. She should sit facing him, he told her, with the glass in her hand and throw water in his face whenever she might see his eyes close longer than to blink. She brought the water, and also a towel for him to use in case she had to use the water.

Twice within the next hour she had to throw water in his face. Both times he'd been talking and had stopped in the middle of a sentence as his eyes went shut. It was six o'clock when it happened the second time; it would be dark within another hour or so. He doubted that he could possibly stay awake even that long, and certainly not much longer.

When he had dried his face with the towel, he stood up, swaying a bit. 'Miss Talley,' he said, 'it's no use going on this way; even if I put carpet tacks on a chair and sit on them I'll lose consciousness eventually. We've got to do one of two things. There's danger in both of them, for you as well as for me, so I'm going to let you decide which we should do.

'One, I leave now while there's time for me to walk to town – or at least to the nearest farm that has a telephone. I'll take the shotgun and leave you the pistol. Maybe I'll make it; maybe we're overestimating the danger and overestimating the range at which the enemy can operate. Anyway, if I do make it I'll see that you're rescued. There'll be state police, several carloads of them with shotguns and tommy guns . . . If I don't get through—'

'No,' Miss Talley said firmly. 'If you go, we both go, and I do the driving. Or afoot, if you think there's any advantage to that. But why would there be?'

'It should keep me awake, for one thing. And for another, I can watch upwards. As I said before, a heavy bird diving from a sufficient height would probably go right through the roof of a car as light as that, and kill whichever one of us it landed on. But your going with me wasn't the alternative to my first suggestion. I don't know whether the alternative is more dangerous, or less.

'It's simply that I go to sleep, here in this room on the sofa, but that we take the precaution of having you tie me up first. There's fifty feet of clothes-line in the kitchen, so you can do a thorough job of it. First, our idea of what may happen to me if I sleep is only a deduction; we can be wrong. Second, if the enemy does take me over, I'll be tied up so he'll be helpless to make me do anything, such as injure you, and also unable to make me kill myself so he'll be free to take another host. And that would mean it would be safe for you to drive into town and bring help.'

'But – what kind of help, if you're—'

'We can't figure that till we see what happens. But if you're the one who gets to town, there'll be no hurry. Get your story – and take my statements with you to supplement it – before the highest authority you can reach. It'll be out of our hands and somebody will have to take over from there. Preferably the FBI – phone them first and try to get either Roger Price or Bill Kellerman on the line; they're both friends of mine and will be more likely to take you seriously. You can remember the names, or do you want me to write them down?'

'Roger Price or Bill Kellerman. I'll remember. But – how would I know it would be safe for me to drive to town? Unless – well, unless once you go to sleep you wake up and act crazy, try to get out of the ropes or – or something like that?'

'If I do that, you'll know, of course. If I don't, you'll have to take the risk of doing what I did a little while ago. Step out on the porch with the shotgun and – well, see if anything attacks you. If nothing does, you'll have to take the chance that nothing will. Or – wait, you don't even have to take the chance. Once I'm tied up, and whether or not I'm still myself, you can just wait it out until the sheriff shows up some-time tomorrow. That's safer for you; I should have thought of it first. I'm so sleepy that I'm not thinking clearly any more.'

'All right,' Miss Talley said. 'I like that better than letting you try to make it to town alone. Or, for that matter, even both of us trying together.'

'I'll get the rope then.'

She went out into the kitchen with him and while he got the length of rope, she got a knife to cut it with.

Back in the living-room Doc took the pistol from his pocket and put it and the ammunition for it and the shotgun on the mantel. He leaned the shotgun against the wall beside the front door. 'Keep all those things out of my reach,' he told her. 'The knife too, once you've finished using it on the rope. Tie my hands first, behind me, then I'll lie down for you to tie my ankles.' He turned his back to her and held his hands behind him for her to work on. 'Listen, if I do go crazy and try to get out of the ropes, don't take any chances on what I might do. Hit me on the head with the pistol butt and knock me out. But try not to kill me; if the enemy is in control of me – and he will be if I try to escape – killing me would free him to take other hosts again and you'd be back where you were before. He might even take you over if you shouldn't be able to stay awake until the sheriff gets here tomorrow.'

Miss Talley was working on the knot. 'Are you sure that this isn't even more dangerous than – than trying to get to town?'

'Of course I'm not sure, but I think so. I'm almost sure that it's safer for you, and not any more dangerous for me.'

'If you think so, all right. Is that tight enough?'

'Perfect. And you've got the knot where I can't reach it with my fingers. All right, I'll lie down now. And I can still force myself to stay awake long enough for you to tie my ankles.'

He did, barely. The moment he approved the job she did on his ankles he sighed and closed his eyes. Instantly he was sound asleep.

Miss Talley stood watching him for a few minutes. And then, because she wanted to know, if possible, whether or not the enemy was in Dr Staunton's mind but was still letting him sleep or pretend to sleep, she picked up the shotgun and opened the door, looking upwards. Something big and black was coming down, diving at her, but she saw that she had time and that stepping back into the house would be safer than raising the gun and taking a shot that could miss, or fail to deflect even if it killed. She stepped back and closed the door just as something heavy thudded to the porch outside the door.

The thing that thudded had been a buzzard, one of several that had gorged themselves on the dead deer and flapped away to sleep in nearby trees. It was the third of these that the mind thing had used.

The mind thing had been annoyed by the unexpected arrival of the school-teacher, Miss Talley. He had been aloft at the time he saw the coming Volkswagen, but had quickly crash-landed and killed his host and taken over the nearest bull. He'd charged it through the fence just after the Volkswagen went by, and followed. His first thought had been to charge and wreck the car, but when Staunton had fired the first barrel of the shotgun at him and he realised that the man had aimed low with intent to cripple rather than to kill, he had changed direction and charged so that Staunton had to shoot to kill in order to save his own life.

Then, back in his own body, the tortoise-like shell hidden under the back steps of the house, he had watched and listened to the conversation between the man and the woman long enough to realise that they knew the futility of their trying to get back to town, or even to a phone, either afoot or in the small car. That, of course, made it unnecessary for him to destroy the car.

He relaxed then and studied them and listened to their conversation, surprised that they had been able to deduce so many things about him, but understanding, after hearing their explanations, how they had been able to do so. It didn't worry him; there was nothing that they could do about it. He didn't have to maintain a host in the air; he knew, of course, whenever one of them planned to attempt leaving and was able to have a bird aloft, usually by the time the door opened.

But then he learned from their conversation that Miss Talley had asked the sheriff to come out. True, she said the sheriff had promised to come tomorrow, but the sheriff could change his mind and come sooner, or send a deputy sooner. And if another car should approach he wanted advance warning so he could deal with the situation. Perhaps it would be better to wreck the car, and kill the occupant if and when he left it, than to let him reach the house alive and reinforce the opposition.

After that, as Staunton or Miss Talley made periodic circuits of the windows of the house, so the mind thing periodically took a flying host aloft to circle high into the sky to scan the road from town and still keep the house under observation, as when out of his own body he could not use his perceptive sense to check on what was going on inside the house. After each flight he had killed the bird by crashing it, and had been instantly back in his shell.

He had been just starting such a flight when Staunton had said he could not possibly stay awake much longer; he knew then it would probably be the last such reconnaisance flight he'd have to make. But because it might be his last, he had circled high to check the road as far as possible. And thus he had not been aware of the final conversation between Staunton and the school-teacher, or the tying up of Staunton.

So he was surprised, when he was just about ready to crash his buzzard host, to see *Miss Talley* step outside alone with the shotgun. Of course he had dived at her immediately, and his buzzard host had died with the impact.

But then he was back in his own shell, as Miss Talley was back in the house, and was even more surprised to discover that his potential host, Staunton, was asleep and tied up in rope. That he was asleep was no surprise, but that he was tied up!

It was devilishly clever, and thwarting. Neither of them had thought of, or at least neither of them had mentioned that idea in any part of their conversation that he had overheard. One of them must have thought of it suddenly, and they had executed it quickly.

Now if he entered Staunton's mind he would be helpless until Staunton's body was untied, and he hesitated and considered. He decided finally that it was safe. The woman couldn't keep Staunton tied up for ever. And if he entered Staunton's mind now but caused Staunton's body to continue to sleep he could make good use of time. He could study Staunton's most intimate thoughts and memories and by the time – say, in the middle of the night – he let Staunton's body awaken, he would be able to act the part of Staunton so thoroughly that Miss Talley would suspect nothing and untie him. And then – but the rest of his plans could also be worked out in the long hours he would be immobile in Staunton's mind while the body slept.

He entered.

And now he encountered something new to him – not in kind, but in degree. Every mind he'd ever entered fought back for a fraction of a second at least. A minor struggle in the case of an animal mind, a severe but brief one in the case of the three human minds he had previously taken over – the two high school boys and the old German farmer.

This fight was no different, except in degree. The struggle lasted for seconds longer than any other he'd engaged in – and during it Staunton was still in partial control of his own body. He fought against what was happening and managed to jerk his body up almost to a sitting position and to gasp out: 'Under steps. Thing like—'

But then it was over; the mind thing was in control.

Doc Staunton lay back and breathed deeply a time or two, and then opened his eyes. They met those of Miss Talley, who was standing by the couch staring down at him. He said, normally and casually, 'think I had a touch of nightmare, Miss Talley. Probably from being overtired. Did I make any noises?'

Miss Talley didn't answer for seconds. Then, very quietly: 'You made noises, Doctor – if you *are* Dr Staunton. You said, and I quote, "Under steps. Thing like—" and that was all. What *was* your nightmare about?'

'Good Lord, Miss Talley. How can I remember, except vaguely that it was something about a charging bull and – oh, yes, in the nightmare I ran and I was trying to crawl under the front steps to hide from it – in the dream I didn't have a gun. I think I can go to sleep again now – and let's hope, no more nightmares.' He closed his eyes.

'Dr Staunton, you told me that you thought "the enemy", as you called it, was nearby and could be hiding inside the house. And that you searched the house for it – which would include any area under the staircase inside. Besides, you didn't say "staircase"; you said "under steps". And there are three steps leading to the front porch and another three leading to the back door. I'm going to look. Now, while it's still light outside.'

'Miss Talley, that's ridiculous. A nightmare—'

But he was talking to empty space. Miss Talley was already out of the front door, taking the shotgun and the pistol with her. And a flashlight; it was still light outside, but might be dim under the steps.

Outside, after looking up and then around to see if anything was about to attack – she didn't really think anything would be, but she had to make sure – she looked under the front steps, using the flashlight. She found nothing, but decided she'd investigate more thoroughly, and maybe dig a bit, after she'd made a quick investigation of the steps at the back of the house. She walked around to the rear.

Nothing was under the back steps either, at first glance; then the flashlight found a spot where the dirt looked as though it might have been dug up and then replaced and patted down. *Yes,* there was the imprint of a hand there, a human hand!

Paying no attention to getting her clothes dirty, she lay flat and wriggled until her head and one arm were under the steps. She clawed and scraped at the area under the hand print. The earth was loose there and moved easily. She felt *something*. It could have been the shell of a turtle – except that turtles do not burrow, especially in dry ground. She came up with something, whatever it was, and pulled it out as she backed away. It was *something* like a turtle except that there were no open places for legs and head and tail—And on second glance it looked – *alien.*

She dropped it in revulsion, put the muzzle of the pistol against the centre of what would have been the carapace, and fired.

Inside the house, Dr Staunton screamed, as though in agony. She ran around to the front – since the back door was bolted – and into the house. She'd forgotten the shotgun but still had the pistol in her hand.

Doc was on the floor instead of on the couch, but he was lying quietly, a peaceful smile – a beatific smile – on his face. He said, 'You did it, Miss Talley. That was *he* and won't the terrestrial doctors have fun dissecting him, the first extra-terrestrial life form they ever have had a chance at. A brain in a shell, and not much more. Not even digestive organs; he absorbed food by osmosis.

'Don't untie me, Miss Talley. It would be all right to, but you can't know it yet. Just let me talk. Lord, do I have things to talk about! And such important things that I feel as though I'll never sleep again.'

He sighed. 'Poor little alien. All he wanted was to get home – but it wouldn't have been good for the human race if he had. You see, Miss Talley, he was in my mind, after that short struggle when I managed to hold him off long enough to get out a few important words – and thank you for interpreting them correctly' – he shivered at the recollection – 'but I was in *his* mind too. I know everything that he knew. Including, although that's a long story, why he chose each of the hosts, human and otherwise, that he used, and the purpose for which he used it, or tried to use it.'

'Where was he from – another planet in the solar system?'

'No, a planet of a very far star. One we'll stay away from for a long, long time. Do you want to know what else I learned, Miss Talley?'

She didn't even have to nod; the expression on her face was answer enough.

Doc said quietly, reverently, 'A science new to us, one we

haven't even suspected. Space travel without tears. We can scratch rockets; they're obsolete. With what I know now, we'll be in space within a year. Colonising anything colonisable within two years – and not only possibly colonisable places in the solar system – anywhere; distance doesn't matter. We can hit a planet of Alpha Centauri – or any other star – as easily as we can move to the moon.

'And, Miss Talley, *anyone* can go – once the bright and strong young spacemen we'll develop have established that a planet is habitable and safe, even for people our age. Miss Talley, will you come with me and be my secretary and good right hand while I work things out?

'And – oh, say three years from now would you like to do a bit of planet-hopping with me? Quick shots to Mars and Venus, say, for a starter – they'll have to be quickies because we'll have to wear space suits – and then – anywhere, anywhere in the universe, or maybe just in the local galaxy for a start, where there are approximately Earth-type planets, ones we can spend at least a few days on without having to live in an artifical environment . . . Where would you like to go first, Miss Talley?'

She believed him, but she'd probably have untied him even if she'd been in doubt. She untied his ankles first and then he rolled on to his side so she could get at the knots on his wrists. He sat up, then moved to the sofa.

He asked, since she hadn't answered his first question – she couldn't; she'd have choked trying – 'Is it a deal, Miss Talley?'

A simple *yes* she could say, and did say, fervently. But Dr Staunton couldn't have heard it; when he'd finished asking his question, and before her quick answer, there intervened – a gentle snore. Dr Staunton was sound asleep.

Miss Talley stared at him for a long moment. Then she went to the door, opened it, and went out on to the porch, carrying no weapon, knowing that she was safe.

She stared up at the sky; it was early dusk and a few stars, the brightest ones, were already visible. Soon there'd be the thousands of visible ones, out of the trillions—

Her life, except for reading, had been dull – but it had not been in vain. She'd still be alive when the human race would begin to become – what the human race *would* become, *must* become. And she'd never need the outlet of reading imaginative literature again; imagination was about to be replaced by here-and-now current reality!

There were more stars visible now, but one of the at-first-visible ones – it was Sirius, she knew – was brighter than any of the others. She stared at it until it blurred and then became invisible because her eyes had filled with tears, tears of a rapture so intense that it was akin to pain.